BI

STEPPING
INTO
TRAFFIC

STEPPING
INTO
TRAFFIC

K.J. Rankin

thistledown press

Thistledown Press Ltd.
410 2nd Avenue North
Saskatoon, Saskatchewan, S7K 2C3
www.thistledownpress.com

Library and Archives Canada Cataloguing in Publication
Rankin, K. J.,1956-, author
Stepping into traffic / K.J. Rankin.

Issued in print and electronic formats.
ISBN 978-1-77187-101-3 (paperback).–ISBN 978-1-77187-102-0 (html).–
ISBN 978-1-77187-103-7 (pdf)

I. Title.
PS8635.A547S74 2016   jC813'.6   C2016-901051-1
C2016-901052-X

Cover and book design by Jackie Forrie
Author photo by John Ngo
Printed and bound in Canada

Canada Council   Conseil des Arts
for the Arts   du Canada

Thistledown Press gratefully acknowledges the financial assistance of
the Canada Council for the Arts, the Saskatchewan Arts Board, and the
Government of Canada for its publishing program.

ACKNOWLEDGEMENTS

Many thanks to my writing friends Pat Bourke, Karen Krossing, Patricia McCowan, Erin Thomas, and Lena Coakley for their invaluable feedback. Thanks as well to Peter Carver and the participants of his Writing for Children workshop who always provided an inspiring oasis. And special thanks go to my editor, Harriet Richards, for her astute guidance, and my sister, Catherine Henderson, for her unflagging support.

One

I'm staring blindly at a pile of fan belts, trying to ignore the acid drip in my stomach, and wishing my head didn't stretch above the store shelves like a beacon. Chris and Alex saunter single file down the auto parts aisle. Chris has on his poker face, meaning he thinks he's pretty cool. He slips his hand inside the trench-style coat he found at Goodwill. As they pass, he whispers, "Got 'em. Let's go." I feel the wire cutters drop into my knapsack, tugging it farther down my back. Now we're ready for the big stuff.

Turning to follow, I step on Alex's heel. "Sorry, man. Didn't see you down there."

Alex doesn't look around. "Watch yourself, asshole." His voice is muffled by the hoodie pulled up from under his leather jacket. He pushes past Chris. "Why'd you have to bring the fuckin' radio tower?"

Chris looks back at me. "Be cool, Sebastian."

"Sure." As if he's ever done anything like this. Has he?

I follow Chris who's following Alex toward the front of the store. No one is supposed to figure out we know each other. Which is funny because I really don't know Alex. I never met him before Chris hooked us up this

7

evening. "Guy's a mastermind at making easy money," he whispered, eyes shining.

I stare down each aisle, afraid I'll catch someone spying on us. Then I spot a security guard — tanker in a blue suit — parked to the right of the doors. I trip over my own toe as Chris and Alex exit. Hands jammed in my pants pockets, I slouch past the checkout and study my soggy runners.

Four more steps. I look up and get caught in an intense eye-lock with the Blue Tanker. Two steps. Eye-lock's over and the automatic doors slide open. One step . . . I'm out!

I stride away from the exit, filling my lungs with the cold January air. That wasn't too bad. Easy, really. As long as you keep your cool. Just like at the electronics 'stuper' store, where Alex scored. Practically filled his knapsack, jacking stuff behind the back of a stunned salesman. Wish I'd gone for it there. It's true — people who work in these giant places couldn't care less. After all, it isn't their stuff. Does anyone really own all that stuff?

I breathe out a cloud of steam. Looking through it, I see Chris and Alex moving past parked cars on their way to the far end of the building.

Goosebumps prickle across my shoulders. Time to bust open the trailer.

The headlights of cars streak by, blurring against the black night.

Why the hell am I here? I just want to go home, sit on the sofa and watch cartoons with little Maggie.

But I told Chris I'm in. I'm not quitting now.

I stuff my hands into the pockets of my lame pleather jacket. Heading away from my best b, I stroll through the busy parking lot then, at the end of the building, jump over a snow bank. A spotlight attached high to the side wall comes on as I slip past. Motion detector.

I check over my shoulder and dodge behind the building.

Chris, Alex, and I meet in front of a long trailer parked against the store's rear wall. Packed snow spreads from there to the back fence. Except for the hum from Lawrence, it's so quiet, we could be in a cemetery. In the dingy light coming from past the fence, I see a chain padlocked through the handles of the trailer's double doors.

Chris slaps my back. "Seb, you the Ice Man! See? Told you it was easy."

I nod, picture a crack in the ice.

Alex says, "Time to pop the motherlode."

Chris' eyes bug out. "Bet this puppy's full of loot that can't wait to be liberated!"

"Puppy?" Alex squints at Chris. "You're a goof."

Chris laughs.

I shuffle my feet, glance around. Wish these guys would whisper. Wish I could see better through the dark.

Alex says, "So, Ice-Cube, you fuckin' frozen or what?"

Little prick. "Yeah. My toes are numb."

He sighs. "Just give me the fuckin' cutters, ya dozer!"

Chris says, "Ouch!"

I fumble with my pack, fish the wire cutters out, and hand them over. "You sure they don't have cameras back here?"

Alex grabs them. "Yeah, I'm sure. Besides, it's dark, duh!"

A muscle in my jaw twitches. "Chris, your *mastermind of making easy money* is seriously starting to bug me."

Chris shrugs, pulls a flashlight from one of his pockets, holds it under his chin, then says, "Mug shot!" It lights up his ghoulish, grinning face. His curls look like horns.

A shiver runs down my spine. "Quit it."

He shines the beam at the chain. "You quit being a girl."

Alex holds the cutters to a link. As he squeezes the blades together, the chain slips out from between them. "Hey, Ice," he says. "Hold the chain."

I look back and forth across the empty yard, strain to hear any sounds besides the cars. It's too quiet.

Chris nudges me. "Come on!"

I grab the chain. My hands are shaking. "Hurry up. I'm freezing."

This time, the cutters slice through. The chain sticks to my palms for an instant before falling loose and clattering against the trailer.

"Yeah!" Chris shoves me out of the way. He grabs one door handle, Alex grabs the other, and they pull. The doors fly open.

Chris shines his light into the empty trailer.

Empty.

A man calls, "Stay right where you are!"

I spin around, adrenalin blazing through me. Five huge guys march toward us, steady as snowploughs.

"We're screwed." Chris looks stunned.

Alex and I take off in different directions.

I'm racing for the fence, my heart hammering like it'll explode and my runners slipping crazily over the packed snow. My knee smacks down on ice, but I push off and scramble ahead, cold air stabbing through my chest. I lunge at the fence then jam the toe of my shoe between the links. I can do this. I'm about to swing my other leg over the top when someone grabs my jacket and yanks me backward.

My hands stick, then rip away from the metal fence. The Blue Tanker steps forward and slams me onto my back where I stay, gasping for air and watching my blood make a black mess on the snow.

Someone says, "Damn kids. Better call the cops."

TWO

"**S**hoplifting! You're lucky Jim made me call a sitter and go fetch you." At least Betty's whispering now we're home. "I'd have left you in jail overnight." She chucks a frozen dinner into the microwave and slams the door.

First food I've seen since lunch. I'm hungry and sore. I peel the useless bandages off my hands, check out the raw stripes stinging across my fingers and palms.

Betty stabs at the oven's control panel, her frizzy hair vibrating. "You've been here for almost a year, and this is the thanks we get?"

Wish she would just shut up.

She pushes another button and the microwave door swings open. "I'll wait to cook your dinner once Jim's here."

I focus on the lumps of dry gum stuck underneath the tabletop, pressing into my knees. At breakfast this morning, I went up on my toes every time Betty's back was turned. My end of the table lifted so's the salt, pepper, and ketchup all shuffled away from me. That got Maggie giggling so she slid right off her chair.

Wish it didn't feel like ancient history now.

Betty yanks open a drawer. "What on earth were you thinking?"

"I don't know." It's not as if I thought I'd get rich. Just tighter with Chris, I guess.

Chris cried when the cops stuffed us into their car. Alex laughed at him.

I felt like barfing.

Betty slaps a fork down on the table. "You want to end up in jail?"

Jail. Shit.

I pick up the fork. Put it down again.

"Because that's where you're headed!"

At the police station, a huge cop with squinty eyes, a thick nose, and wide, pitted cheeks shoved me into a room with two chairs and a dinky table. You're not going to be seeing your buddies for a long time, *he said.*

For a second, the grey walls moved, like they were liquid.

The cop said, Sit.

I dropped. Almost missed the chair.

He wedged himself into the other chair. His slab of a head pushed forward. Whose idea was it? Where else did you try? I bet you're pretty good at this, eh? Do it all the time, eh?

When I said I never really stole anything, ever, he grabbed the sides of the desk and shoved his ugly face into mine. You're lying.

He made me give him my belt and shoelaces, said I should reflect *on my answers, then left me alone.*

After I stopped shaking, I started wondering why I was there. And why I'd never tried stealing before. 'Specially back in grade seven, when practically everyone was a klepto. I figured I'd still believed that Mom and Dad were always watching.

"Seb, stop tapping that fork. Are you listening to me?"

Surprised to find it in my hand, I put the fork down, focus on Betty. "Yeah, I'm listening." Jim's draining the bathtub now. Wish he'd hurry up. I'm starving.

"I've got Little J and Maggie to think of, you know. They look up to you."

Everyone looks up to me. I'm a fuckin' giraffe. Probably why we got caught.

"You hear me?"

"Yeah."

Thumb-sucking Little J only crawls my way when I've got candy. His big sister, Maggie, is different, though. The little nutbar's all over me the second I walk through the door. *Can I have a horsey ride?* Gets me to crawl around, snorting and neighing, while she sits on my back, whacking my butt and shrieking, "Giddy up, Red!"

But when I came in after the cop station and whinnied, all she did was stick her tongue out and go back to watching cartoons. Guess she knew her mom was mad at me.

Talk about getting kicked when you're down.

Betty drops a serviette on the table then pulls a pack of cigarettes from her sweater pocket. She smacks one out and lights it, staring at me the whole time. She'd probably rather smoke than eat. I glance at the frozen dinner in the open microwave.

Betty takes a drag and blows out a long, thin stream of smoke. It catches on a draft from the cracked window and snakes through the kitchen to the back door. I hate that my coat, on a hook there beside everyone else's, always stinks of smoke.

Betty sucks on her cigarette, eyes narrowed to tiny blue blades. "You're setting a bad example for Maggie and Little J."

"No way!" I push away from the table. The legs drop to the floor with a bang I didn't mean to make. I stand, jittery. "They don't know. Do they?"

Something's different about Betty. Her stare's scarier than the cop's. She going to belt me?

For a moment, I can't breathe. I choke out, "I'm sorry."

She takes another puff. "I can't trust you anymore, Sebastian. I want you out."

She glares, smoke filling the space between us, her lips a thin, mean line.

I scramble for words to change her mind. "I won't do it again."

She turns to the sink.

"I promise," I say to her back.

Jim steps into the kitchen, drying his hands on a towel. "Got them both in bed now, Bet." He tosses the towel over the back of a chair.

I gotta work on Jim. He'll listen.

Betty squashes her cigarette on a plate by the sink. "Jim, you're always leaving towels in here! I hate that!" She slams the microwave door again and starts my dinner cooking.

"Take it easy, babe," Jim says. "I'll put it away right now." He balls up the towel, stands in the archway to the living room, and then rifles it across the corner of the room. The towel flies through the open bathroom door, hits the far wall, and slides down onto a hook above the tub.

He looks at me with a cocky grin.

15

I force a smile. "Man, you're good at that. You'd have made a great quarterback."

"Yeah, eh?" Jim drops onto a chair. "I do have a good arm."

He tilts his head to the side and grins up at me. "We knew you were a scrapper, boy. We didn't know you were a thief."

"I'm not, really. And I never start fights." I talk fast. "I never actually lifted anything. Chris picked up the wire cutters."

Jim's hand thumps the table, almost makes me jump like the fork. "Who are you trying to kid? You got caught in the act! B and E. Possession of burglary tools." At least he's still smiling — sort of. "Hell, you're going to court."

The smell of meat loaf mixes with stale smoke.

Betty says, "Jim, tone down! The kids."

Maggie and Little J share the bedroom past the bathroom, but in this joint, if someone farts everyone hears it. If Maggie didn't know why her mom was pissed off before, she does now. Unless she's asleep. I hope she's asleep.

Jim looks at Betty. "Haven't most kids outgrown stealing by sixteen?"

"Stop it, Jim. It's wrong at any age."

The microwave beeps.

"I'm really sorry, Jim." My chest feels too tight. "I was stupid. It wasn't my idea."

"So what?" Betty pushes past me, thumps a tiny tray with two slices of meat loaf, peas, and potato on the table. "Eat."

"Thanks, Betty." Maybe she'll change her mind. "You always buy the best." I drop back onto the chair and reach for the tray.

Jim grabs my wrist. "Hey! What happened to your hand?"

I pull my arm away. "Nothing."

"Hold on!" Jim examines my cuts. "Betty, what the hell happened?"

Betty sighs. "He tried to climb a fence. His hands stuck on the frozen metal when they pulled him down."

Jim releases my hand, his face twisting with disgust. "Are you kidding? He ran?"

My left ear heats up. "Jim, I didn't want to . . . "

"To what? Get in trouble?" Jim cracks his knuckles. "You screw up, you gotta man-up!"

"I know." I swallow, but my mouth is dry. "I'm sorry."

Jim nods. "You better be."

Betty slips onto the chair beside him, puts her hand on his thigh. "We've got to talk."

Jim frowns. "We are, Bet."

"Just you and me."

Jim sighs. "You better wait in your room for a bit, Seb."

"But, my dinner's — "

"But nothing," Betty says. "Now."

What the hell? I stand. "I've never screwed up before! You can't . . . "

"Don't you shout at him!" Betty's eyes flash.

"I'm not!"

Betty jumps up, jabs her finger into my stomach. "You think you can scare us?"

"No! I'm — " For an instant, I see Psycho-Dad closing a curtain, his lips pressed so tight they disappear in the bloodless skin bubbled around them. "I'm just — "

"About to start punching," she says, staring at my white-knuckled fists.

"No!" I shout.

"Take it easy, Seb," Jim says. "Betty — "

"You do something then!" Betty shoves his chair.

"Listen, Jim," I say, leaning closer, so he has to listen.

Betty says. "Jim, why aren't you — "

"Please, just listen." I grab his sleeve. "It won't happen again. I mean I won't — "

"Don't just sit there!" Betty yanks Jim's arm from my grasp.

Jim smacks the table. "Stop it!"

Betty and I freeze.

"Seb." He jerks his head towards the living room. "Your room. Right now. Move."

My stomach one giant knot, I reel out of the kitchen. I drop onto my bed, lie on my back staring at the little holes in the ceiling tiles.

"We've got our own to think of, Jim. We need the money, but . . . "

I may as well be stretched out right in the stinkin' kitchen. I can tell by the breaks in her voice that Betty's smoking another cigarette.

I can hear Jim scratch his head. Means he's thinking.

"He's too much trouble, Jim."

"He said it won't happen again."

My blood thuds in my ears, mixes with their voices.

"Don't be so naïve. This probably isn't the first time."

"I just feel sorry . . . "

Is that a sob? Here she goes. "It's not fair to Maggie and Little J."

"Ah, come on, baby. Calm down." I bet she's sitting on his lap now.

More crying. I'm screwed. Unless Jim's —

"Stop that, Betty. We'll get them to send another one — a younger one. Everything's going to be okay, babe."

I suck in my breath. So . . . that's it . . . I'm out.

"Okay." She blows her nose. "You're right."

Feels like there's something stuck in my throat. I swallow.

At least they never hit me. Guess I'm too big for that now.

But, shit. It's like I just got stabbed in the gut.

I roll onto my stomach. Punch my fist into my pillow.

Seven "homes" in eight years.

What's next?

Three

First time I smell aftershave in ages. It makes my nose itch. The barber snips the back-fringe of an old balding guy and sings some corny 'O, sol-a-me-o." I glance in the mirror at Hassles reading her magazine beside me, then at my crazy curly hair.

The barber smiles into the mirror and tells the old guy, "Your lady's going to love this." Once, before I got busted, I asked Maggie, *Do you like my hair, or do I look like a clown?* She looked up, all serious, and said, *You look like a clown and I love it!*

Shit — I'm not going to cry over that little kid now.

Hassles lowers the magazine, peers at me through oversized glasses. "Are you okay, Seb?"

I nod.

She looks at the barber. "Vince knows what he's doing. You'll look good with it short."

"I guess." My hair's finally as long as Chris', but it doesn't matter anymore.

"Besides, Ms. Chen said you need it cut for court."

"Yeah." My stomach knots.

"Ms. Haslett, I'm ready for the young man," the barber calls.

Sometimes I wonder if I'm the only one who thinks *Hassles* is a better fit than her real name. "Okay." She smiles. "This is Sebastian."

I drop into the red swivel chair, watch Vince happily slash almost a year's worth of wishing, and in less than twenty minutes I'm folding myself back into Hassles' compact car, a chill prickling my naked neck.

She stretches the seatbelt over her pot and then pulls away from the curb saying, "Now we're off to your new home."

Home. Using that word always makes me feel like a liar.

"Sebastian, I've got something important to say." She's using her official voice. "Have I got your attention?"

"Uh-huh."

"You know that when you're eighteen Children's Service Centre is no longer responsible for you."

Everything under my ribcage drops a couple inches. "Yeah." That's a hard one to forget — being all on my own.

"I'm sorry that the Kirbles didn't give you a second chance."

"Jim would've."

Hassles shrugs. "But now, if Mrs. Ford decides she can't live with you, your next and last stop until you turn eighteen will be an open-custody facility."

"Huh?"

She sighs. "A group home."

I feel my scalped hair stand up. Chris' older brother spent time in a group home. Said they should be called grope homes since most of the guys there are either on you for sex or whatever's in your pockets.

Hassles stops for a red light. "And don't forget, if the police pick you up for anything before your court date, Children's Services Centre cannot save you from spending at least one night in jail." She glances my way.

"I know that." As if I need reminding. Just last week when we were at the lawyer's, Ms. Chen basically said that, one way or another, I'll end up in jail — juvie. Glad I don't see her again till court.

Crap. I gotta quit thinking about court.

By the time we pull up in front of foster home eight, I've got this surreal sort of déjà vu feeling. But then, lots of neighbourhoods look alike in this city. Maybe my strange feeling is just nerves, or my head's fresh overexposure.

The driveway ends at a sturdy garage. Everything looks recently painted. The porch railing doesn't have any rust spots, and curtains that match hang in the windows on either side of the front door. It all looks so perfect.

An image of Psycho-Dad, eyes bulging, belt swinging bursts into my brain. What if Ford's a control freak too?

"Okay, Seb. This is it." Hassles turns off the car. "You've got to do your part to make this work. Mrs. Ford's getting on but she's a great lady."

"Oh?" I'm riveted to my seat. Even burping without permission sent Psycho-Dad ballistic. "It looks too perfect." Hassles already has one leg out, but she stretches a thick arm past me to push my door open. "Don't be silly. You really don't want to screw this up."

Instead of *Shut up!* I say, "No, I don't."

I haul myself out of the car, yank my knapsack from the back, and follow Hassles onto the porch. A short, grey-haired lady opens the front door and smiles. A million wrinkles gather around her mouth and eyes. "Welcome, Sebastian! I'm Margaret Ford."

Getting on? She's ancient! I can't think of a thing to say, so I just shut my mouth — which has fallen open — and nod.

Hassles shakes her hand. "It's nice to see you again, Margaret."

"And you, Ms. Haslett."

"Please, call me Anne."

"Sebastian, Anne, come on in." Ford steps back so that we can move into the entryway. "Leave your shoes right there." She points at a plastic mat with a pair of boots on it. "And hang your jackets on the coat tree."

The house smells clean — reminds me of Psycho-Dad again. Down the hall, opposite a side table with a big, old telephone attached to a stretchy cord, an opening leads to the living room. It's filled with flowery furniture that's gotta be even older than the old lady. The TV looks antique, too.

"Anne, why don't you stay here while I show Sebastian his room?"

Hassles drops into a purple-and-green chair and I follow Ford down a short hall.

My new bedroom's smaller than the one at Jim and Betty's, but way nicer. There's a window, plus a closet and a desk. And the bed — no cot or sagging mattress — looks 'bout the best yet, with a real wood frame. A chin-up bar is fastened near the top of the closet door. "Cool room."

"It was my son's, a long time ago now."

"Where'd he go?" I ask, wondering where I'll sleep when he shows up.

She sighs. "He moved out to Alberta after high school."

"I heard that's where the jobs are."

"Yes." She gazes around the room, her hands together, one thumb rubbing the other till she sees me looking.

Arthritis? Reminds me of Grumpy-Gram from foster-family three.

"You can unpack later, Sebastian."

I dump my bag on the dresser. My stuff won't fill more than two of the drawers.

Back in the living room, Hassles taps a folder lying on the glass-topped coffee table. "I've got a bit of paperwork to go over with you, Margaret."

Ford smiles. "Of course. But can I get you both something to drink first?"

Nice — but my last four foster parents all sucked up to Hassles.

"And since it's getting late, I ordered some pizza — an early dinner, if you're hungry, Sebastian."

"Pizza?" I sit up straighter. "I'm always hungry."

Hassles sighs.

Ford's still smiling. "Then I'll do my best to fill that hollow leg."

Bet her tone changes by breakfast tomorrow.

After she comes back with our drinks, Ford tells Hassles that she's gone into semi-retirement. "After thirty years of nursing, I'm due for a break, Anne."

Hassles nods. "I can imagine. So you're freelance nursing now?"

Ford smiles. "I guess you could call it that."

No one says the obvious: that now she's desperate for CSC money.

Stepping into Traffic

When the pizza arrives, Ford gives her version of the speech that by now I figure must come from some CSC first meeting manual: *We're in this together. It's a two-way street.* Blah, blah, blah. Bunch of hypocrites.

The pizza's nearly demolished when Hassles says, "Seb, would you like to explore your new neighbourhood while Mrs. Ford and I take care of this paperwork?"

I head out with the last slice, wondering what Hassles will tell the old lady about me.

"Be back within an hour," she calls.

❧

As I gaze down the street, there's still something pulling my strings. It's like I've forgotten something or lost something, or . . . I don't know.

A skinny mutt passes, sniffing along the curb. It's grey, like Ford and her house.

I take a bite of cold pizza — probably the best food I'll get here.

The dog sits on the road in front of me, whines. It's a rat-tail, long-neck, racing type — only bit smaller.

"Get lost."

It licks its lips, shuffles its butt closer, sad eyes staring me down.

"Oh, all right." My last bite is barely airborne when the dog — all ribs and sinew — leaps, snatches, and swallows it in one smooth move. It starts staring again.

"Should've chewed that, buddy. Nothing good lasts long."

The dog tilts his head like he's listening.

"Yep. I screwed up."

Dog tilts his head the other way.

"Maggie, Jim, even Betty — closest I've come to belonging since . . . " I pet the top of his head, "Can't talk about that." Dog frowns — a good listener. "And my best friend. Won't see him again till court. Then, who knows?"

The mutt yawns.

"Okay. Time to check out the 'hood."

As I head down the block, the dog slinks along behind me.

"Go home."

He doesn't.

After a few boring blocks, I'm ready to turn around when I see a house that stops me. It's farther back and way older than its neighbours. Black shutters and painted white-brick walls. The covered porch has a friendly sort of sag. Even though I can't make out the door knocker, I'd bet it's a lion's head.

I gaze at the house. Out of line. Out of time.

All at once, I feel as though I've taken a body blow. Memories explode in my head and I shut my eyes to see them better.

Mom on the porch. Reading about Max and his monsters.

Dad leaning against the post, eyes closed. Me waiting — ready to run. *What time is it, Mr. Wolf?*

Mom at the door, waving. *See you later, alligator!*

Mom. Dad. God, I want them so bad, I think my chest's going to cave.

I can't breathe; the sweet memories stab.

"Excuse me! Are you all right?"

My eyes blink open.

A lady stares from halfway across the front yard. "I can call 911." She holds up a phone.

"No." I swipe a hand over my face, surprised to find myself kneeling on the cold, wet grass. "I'm okay."

The front door is open now. A little girl 'bout the size of Maggie watches as she hangs from the door handle, feet tucked up behind her.

"Sorry — I mean, if I scared you," I say, pushing myself to my feet.

The lady steps a little closer, her head tilted, eyebrows scrunched together. "Are you sure you're okay?" Beside her, the skinny dog tilts its head, too. Her dog?

"I'm sure." My eyes lock on the tiny garden. Mom's flower beds, with peonies so big I could hide under them; the endless grass I raced over with my kite — where'd it all go? "The yard shrank," I say. "Or, I grew."

"Oh!" The lady lowers the phone. "Did you live around here?"

I nod, my brain in a haze.

"The property was subdivided." She points at the houses beside mine. "They're taking up the old yard." She smiles. "Where did . . . "

"I've gotta go." I let my feet decide which way. When I glance back, the lady's closing the front door.

The dog's following me again.

I take a deep breath.

My feet have their own plan.

Four

As my feet lead the way to my old school, memories of Mom and Dad fill my brain. Thinking on them more than I have in ages, I realize they made the me I used to be. The one — I know now — I want to be.

I run down the first block, around the corner. The dog lopes ahead as I jog up Madill, way less steep now than when I was little. At the top, I pass the old skate park, deserted now, and my feet take a right. Glancing at houses as I run, names begin to slip over my lips. Tommy Lei, Dace Zaks, Glen Clarke, and Mo Jeewa. Old Man Matson. The Jacksons. Are my old friends still here?

Rounding the final bend, my heart thumps against my ribs. There it is! I slow to a walk, catch my breath. Fairhaven Public School: big windows, cheerful red-brick walls, and those huge trees that we rested under on hot, sweaty days.

A rusted Chevy sits, lonely, in the parking lot. As I wander toward the playground around back, a floodlight above the side door comes on with a soft *pop*.

It's not dark, but for one sickening moment, I'm back sneaking around scared with Chris and Alex in the quiet cold behind Crappy Tire.

The dog sniffs at the garbage bin beside the field. The field looks lonely, too, and a little smaller, but it still stretches to two battered baseball cages and a long chain-link fence.

I tell myself for the millionth time: there's no turning time back.

A metal door clunks open behind me and a man in green coveralls backs through it. He holds a jumble of keys in one hand, a hat in the other. He slides the hat on, locks the door, and then turns.

"Mr. Frogley!" His name shoots out of my mouth.

"Jesus!" He reels back, slaps his palm against the brick wall. "You scared the bejeebers out of me, boy."

"Sorry." He's way shorter than he used to be.

"What the heck?"

"It's just . . . you're still here."

"Well, don't tell anyone." He drops the bundle of keys into a pocket, making his coveralls sag. "I'll have the union on my back. Besides, I'm on my way now. Do I know you?"

"I mean, I remember you from ages ago."

Mr. Frogley squints. "Ages, eh? I suppose you were here when this place was an elementary school?"

"Huh?" I look around. A sign fills the window of the side door: "*Continuing Education Centre*." I feel a fresh stab of longing. "Guess that means it's for adults now?"

He nods. "What's your name, boy?"

"Sebastian Till."

Mr. Frogley shoves his hat up his forehead and smiles. I can see why we used to think he was named after Kermit the Frog.

"Sebastian. Sure, I remember you! Why, 'cept for puttin' on a few feet, you've barely changed. I even remember

29

your mother. She volunteered here a lot. You got her red hair." His face goes all serious. "I was sure sorry."

I swallow. "Thanks."

"Real good people, your folks." He clears his throat. "So, what you doing back here, Sebastian?" He leans against the door, as if he has time to listen.

"It's Seb, now." Feeling a wobble in my voice, I gaze at the parking lot and wait till my insides settle. "I just moved back into the neighbourhood. Thought I'd see what's new."

"Well," Mr. Frogley says, "seeing as you're back now, you gotta come visit me regular. Okay, Seb?" He nods.

"Okay." Probably not.

As we head toward the Chevy, I look around for the dog, but it's gone.

"Can I give you a lift?" Mr. Frogley asks.

"No, thanks."

He reaches to shake hands and grips mine, his calluses rough against my skin. After easing himself into the car, he says, "I hope to see you soon, Seb!" Streetlights flicker on as he pulls out of the parking lot.

I take a last look at the school. I remember running here every morning, playing Knights and Dragons, tag, soccer, swinging my way through funny square dances, and laughing at Adam Bambro's crazy stories.

I jog back to Mrs. Ford's. Maybe, for once, there'll be someone I know at my new school.

I haven't gone two blocks when I find the skinny grey dog loping along beside me. He looks up at me, black lips stretched above his gums like he's smiling. I can't help smiling back.

We run through the streetlights' faint yellow pools together.

Five

The first week at my new school is crap. I only make three positive IDs out of over seven hundred students.

When I say 'hi' to my grade-three reading buddy, her eyes nearly fall out. "Sebastian? You disappeared." She gives her head a quick shake. "Oh, yeah. I remember. You've gotta tell me what you've been up to sometime. Later. Take it easy, eh?" She practically runs away.

Jimmy Ng, third grade four square king, says, "Who? Sorry man," when I introduce myself at the end of my first class with him. Then he takes off, too.

A guy I played Knights and Dragons with all through junior and senior kindergarten chews his bottom lip for about five seconds before saying, "I don't think I know you."

Death's a downer. Besides, my old friends are right. They don't know me anymore. And I don't want to talk about everything — anything — that's happened since I was seven. It just makes me feel like a loser.

Beginning of week two, I'm zoning out in Geography. I really couldn't shiv a git about anything Mr. Walter is saying. And from the look of it, neither could he — slumped against the wall, eyes half shut, droning on about the Ice Age. Should be called Waldozer.

The room? An even bigger joke. This windowless hole had to be the janitor's closet before they tacked a black-board on one side and a map on the other. It's getting warmer and stuffier every minute. Kind of — what's it called? — *ironic* that today's topic is about ice.

I glance at my palms. A few faint lines are all that's left of my frozen fence climb.

I'm about to crash when a chick's sexy voice pulls me back.

"Mr. Walter, could you open the door?"

She's right behind me. Turning around to check her out, I nearly gasp. She's gorgeous! How did I miss her?

"Good idea." Waldozer opens the door. "Aren't we lucky you've honoured us with your presence today, Tiff?"

Someone whispers, "Burned."

Eyes narrowed, Tiff watches Waldozer and twists her shiny hair into a ponytail. Her lips part. As the tip of her tongue peeks out between them, she flips the ponytail up. I turn in my seat a little more. She sticks a pencil in her hair, holding it in place. Amazing. Her lips pucker. I imagine them pressed against mine. She sighs. A puff of minty air floats by. My heart is pounding all over the place. My left ear starts to burn. I whip back around before the rest of me overheats, too.

I could use some of Waldozer's ice right now.

After class I grab my coat and move with the herd of kids streaming out of school into the chilly air of a quiet side street, because that's what Tiff does.

My gaze is pinned to the back of her green sweater. Still, I can't help noticing her long legs that stretch up to . . . perfection.

You're the most beautiful girl in the world. Too much. *I'd follow you anywhere.* Creepy? *Hi. I'm new here.* Needy. *Mind if I copy your geography notes?* Nerdy. *Good idea back there — opening the door.* Boring.

Everyone heads for the main street where a tiny plaza with a convenience store and a pizza place is just three short blocks from school. I've gone half a block when I bump into something and a guy says, "Hey! Watch it!"

I glance down at an angry face above a preppy jacket. "Sorry, man. Didn't see you." My goddess in green is getting way ahead.

"So try watching where you're going." The guy slams my stomach with open palms.

"What the hell?" I stagger backward, feel a jab at my back.

"Excuse me!" a girl shouts from behind. Something thumps on the ground.

Preppy guy's fists jerk up, like he's wired too tight. "What's your problem, Stilts?"

"*My* problem?"

Tiff's green sweater disappears in the jumble of guys and girls crowded together at the main-street traffic light.

My fingers are itching to make fists. "I don't need trouble, but you're lookin' for it."

A frizzy-haired beanpole of a girl steps from behind me and then slides into the space between me and this guy. "Cool it, Markus."

She's taller than Markus and her mass of black curls blocks my view, but after a few seconds he marches away.

The girl holds her hand up after him, fingers fanned wide. "*Sto thialo, pousti!*"

"Huh?"

She turns and looks up from under thick, black eyebrows. "He's a jerk." Then she kneels to collect some books scattered over the sidewalk.

"Guess I did that," I say. "Sorry. Short guys are always looking to hook me."

She shrugs. "The sidewalk's dry, so no damage done."

I help gather the books. "What does stow the al — whatever you said, mean?"

"If I wanted everyone to know, I'd say it in English." She winks. "My advice?" She pushes her crazy hair back. Soon as she takes her hand away, it springs over her face again, cartoon-like. Almost makes me laugh. "Avoid Markus. He's usually hopped up on something."

"Probably why he acted like a robot."

"Could be. By the way, I'm Nina."

"Seb."

"Well. See you around, Seb." She rushes away, her books tucked under a long, skinny arm, and calls, "Hey, Matt!"

A guy eating a bag of chips on his way to the main street slows for her.

I'm at the rear of the pack now. I look back to the school. Nothing says *loser* louder than sitting alone in a cafeteria.

Seeing a small forest of evergreens between the school field and a railway line, I head for a spot I can eat without being seen. I tell myself that if Markus hadn't been in my way, I'd probably be eating with the girl of my dreams.

Stepping into Traffic

Ford is putting on her coat when I get home from school.

"I'm on my way to run some errands. I got backed up because I couldn't say no to a short shift at the Walk-In Clinic today."

"No problem. I'll probably go for a jog or do some homework." Not. It'll be nice without the old lady bugging me with stories about her dumb day or questions about mine.

"There's a brisket in the slow cooker. I'll be home by seven thirty at the latest to eat with you."

"Cool." I have no clue what a brisket is.

"Oh! I almost forgot. I've budgeted for you to buy a cold drink every school day." Ford peers into her purse and then pulls out two toonies. "These will cover the rest of this week."

This foster-parent first leaves me almost speechless. "Thanks!"

"You're welcome. And I think we should go shopping for some clothes for you sometime soon so that we're not doing laundry every other day."

"Sure. Betty liked Value Village better than Goodwill." Not. I like Value Village better, but it's more expensive.

"I prefer Buyers' Best. But, we'll figure that out later." Ford smiles. "I'll be back in a bit."

Buyers Best. Brand new clothes? Amazing — another first.

I get lucky searching the fridge for snack material. A ham sandwich sure beats peanut butter, the one foster family constant. If Ford's getting me new clothes, maybe I won't catch shit for helping myself to the good stuff.

Downing my snack at the kitchen table, I picture me and Tiff together. But who am I kidding? It's not as if I'd ever say anything to her, really. My sex life exists only in my head, and my hand.

I grab a carton of milk and wander into the living room, where I guzzle it down while flipping through the TV channels. Jeopardy, City News, Road Runner, Judge Judy. I stop there. Judge Judy's feathery, blonde hair looks like Chris', 'cept his is longer.

"Look in my eyes!" the judge yells at some poker-faced dude. Her own eyes bulge.

I miss Chris. The police said no getting together before the trial, but who'd know? Still, it's two hours on transit back to the east end.

Judge Judy's voice gets louder. "You've got to take responsibility for your actions. What were you thinking, sir?" She looks ready to kill. The camera cuts back to the now spluttering dude, and I click off the TV. Suddenly, it feels as though the milk I drank is curdling.

I wonder if Chris is worried as me about court.

The cops never said anything about talking to each other.

I call his home, wishing he had a cell phone. Wishing I did, too.

His mom answers. "He ain't here, Sebastian."

"Can I leave my number?"

Silence. She hung up.

I hate telephones.

I can't see Chris, and suddenly I don't wanna sit home alone.

Putting the milk away, I spot an open package of wieners. I grab one and head outside.

It's snowing, big flakes that disappear seconds after hitting the ground.

I haven't been outside more than a minute when, quiet as a shadow, the grey mutt shows up. He's been doing that more and more often. I crouch down. "Knew I'd see you." He rests his muzzle on my knee. I give his head a two-handed rub.

"Your favourite, eh? Your ribs are stickin' out as much as ever. You cold? Bet you're on your own, eh? Me too."

He bolts down half the wiener, tail wagging, then bumps his nose against my knee and looks around, like he's ready for action. "Wanna go for a walk? See where my life started? Eh, boy? It might hurt again, but — "

I lob the rest of the meat at him. "Come on. I've been stalling for too long."

Psyched, I stride through the fat snowflakes to my only real home. In front of the house, I focus, trying to remember the rooms inside. Like last time, my parents' voices and other images creep back, and I hold onto each memory, like an algebra formula, till it's stuck in my mind.

Mom talking to her plants.

Dad dancing Mom around the living room.

Being snuggled safe between them on the couch as flying monkeys frighten Dorothy on TV.

The dog bounds around me, snapping at the falling snowflakes. Reminds me of trying to catch them on my tongue as a kid.

The little girl appears at a window. She waves. I wave back and then take off.

Like last time, my feet turn to Fairhaven. "Hey, Skinny!"

The dog wags his tail.

"You like that name?"

He barks.
"Guess we will go visit Mr. Frogley again, Skinny."
I stick out my tongue, catch a snowflake first try.
"And on Saturday, maybe I'll visit Maggie."

Six

Saturday, as the eastbound bus grinds closer to the Kirbles, I get around to imagining Betty's reaction when she sees me. That puts a knot in my stomach; so instead, I think on Mr. Frogley — how easy it's been to hang with him.

Friday, we shovelled the walkways after another dump of snow, and he talked more about Mom — the time he told her Canadian winters made him miss Jamaica. I never knew that Mom gave him a pair of second-hand skates and some woollen socks. *These should help you learn to love winter,* she'd said. He still wears the skates and plays on an old-timers' hockey team now.

It's amazing hearing stories about Mom from Mr. Frogley. He saw her so differently than I could as her little kid.

A voice announces my stop and suddenly I'm frozen — can't even make myself pull the stop cord. Bitchy Betty and Ford would both have said 'no' to this trip if they'd known about it.

But as the bus slows for another passenger, I remember the bag of candy for Maggie, and pat the pocket it's in. I hope Ford doesn't find out that I spent my milk money on candy and public transit.

When the back door opens, I lunge for the exit, and then jump over a slush puddle onto the sidewalk at the corner of Kingston and Tidemore.

I've been gone from this neighbourhood five weeks. It feels like ages. And it feels like yesterday. The old strip of used car lots, fast food joints, and a couple palm readers looks pretty good.

Five doors along Tidemore, Jim and Betty's semi looks same as always.

Two short blocks away, a couple people turn onto Chris' street. Maybe he will, too.

I wait for two more people to walk down it. Count three more. Then another four.

I'm an idiot. Chris isn't going to just stroll by.

I head down Tidemore. Maggie's rusted tricycle takes up half the front porch. The driveway's a mess of melting slush. A thin strip of white snow next to the neighbour's hedge has a line of tiny boot prints, all neatly heel to toe.

That's gotta be Maggie. Pretending to walk a tightrope?

I take a deep breath, do the porch stairs in one step, slip past the trike, and then hit the doorbell.

After a minute, no one's answered. I press my ear to the door, then push the bell again. It definitely works. I peer through a slit in the sheets Betty uses as curtains on the living room window. Useless.

But, just in case they missed the bell, I hop the porch railing onto the driveway.

I spy through the side door's plastic-covered window at a row of empty coat hooks. My jumble of nerves flatlines. I won't see any of them.

I try the door handle and nearly jump when it opens. Jim must have been last out. No way would Betty forget to lock up.

I look through the tidy kitchen to the living room. I could slide in. Leave the candy on the table. See if anyone has moved into my room.

I let out a breath, shut the door, and slog back to the front of the house. Melting snow dribbles from the porch.

I really am an idiot. Why did I think they'd be home?

After stuffing the candy into the mail slot, I'm trudging back up Tidemore when the Kingston Road bus stops. A guy wearing a trench coat and messy blond hair leaps through the doors and over the same puddle I did.

"Yo!" I pick up my pace. "Chris!"

He gapes around, sees me coming at him, and cracks his goofy grin. "Seb! My man! What's up, bald-o?"

I laugh. "Good to see you, bro! Hardly bald. Bet your hair's gonna go, too, before court."

I reach him just as his mother — all in red and about as wide as she is tall — clumps off the bus straight into the puddle.

"What the . . . ?" She bends forward to see her feet, then steps onto the sidewalk frowning at me as though it's my fault she got two soakers.

I try to look serious. "Hi, Mrs. Hendrick. I — "

"You boys know you ain't supposed to be together."

I blink. "But, this wasn't — "

"Sebastian." Mrs. Hendrick's red mitten pops up like a stop sign. "You gotta wait till after the trial, or there'll be trouble."

"I just came to visit my — "

41

"I got respect for the law, even if you don't." Mrs. Hendrick glances around. "Now get, Seb, before *I* call the cops."

Chris snorts. "You wouldn't."

"Don't tempt me."

"But, Mrs. Hendrick . . . "

She shakes her head, grabs Chris' elbow, and steers him away.

Chris mumbles, "See ya, Seb."

I'm looking after them when the bus back to the subway comes flying along Kingston. I dodge across three lanes of traffic then watch my ride speed by in the fourth.

Tromping back to the subway in slush-splattered clothes and glancing over my shoulder so I don't miss the next bus, I hear a voice screech, "Look, Mommy! It's Red."

Maggie! She's running straight for me, her blue toque bobbing. Amazing — Chris *and* Maggie showing up. Maybe I'm not such an idiot after all.

Betty follows, muscling a stroller full of Little J and two grocery bags around a puddle.

"This is great!" I laugh and grab Maggie's outstretched arms then swing her around, her boots right off the ground.

"Put her down." Betty's voice could frost windows.

I set Maggie down on the sidewalk, keeping hold of one hand in case she's dizzy. Little J smiles up at me and reaches his arms out like he wants a swing, too.

"Hi Betty!" I'm still smiling. "So, how're you all doing? I was just at your place. Thought I'd missed everyone. Want me to carry those bags for you?" I'm babbling.

"Where'd your hair go, Red?" Maggie asks.

"Hair Fairy stole it."

She laughs.

Betty's tiny smile matches her narrowed eyes. "What's going on, Sebastian?"

"I just came by to say hi." My smile feels like work now.

"You came all the way from the west end just to say *hi*?"

I nod. Her face looks tight enough to sliver ice.

Maggie grabs my hands. "Dizzy me again!"

Betty glances at the kids. "You know I don't want you around them."

I feel my ear turning red, as though it agrees.

Maggie shouts, "Dizzy me up, dizzy me down! I like zooming 'round and 'round. That's Red's poem, Mommy. He made it for me!"

I give her shoulder a squeeze. "We made it together, Maggie."

She nods. "I said, *Dizzy me!*"

Betty grabs Maggie's wrist. "Now we've said *hi*, it's time to go."

"But, I just — "

"Save it, Sebastian." Her lips press into the thin mean line I've seen before. "Seb's in a hurry, Maggie. He'll swing you another time."

"I want to play with Red." Maggie's bottom lip bulges.

"Come on, Betty. Can't I just — "

"I've a mind to call Ms. Haslett, tell her you're harassing us."

"But I'm not!"

Maggie starts crying, Little J splutters, and I just stand there like a dope as Betty drags them away.

I am not going to cry.

And sure as hell won't put Maggie through that again.

Another subway-bound bus roars past.

I've just closed the front door when Ford calls, "Come here, Seb. We need to talk."

I shuck off my coat and shoes, then drag myself into the kitchen. I'm so tired of this crappy day I don't care what's on her mind. She's sitting at her little table with a pot of tea and some cinnamon buns. They smell good.

"Will you have some tea? I just made a fresh pot."

"Sure." I drop into my chair. "I haven't had tea since . . . " An image of Mom flashes through my mind. *Tea with your milk and sugar?*

I clear my throat. "I haven't had tea in ages."

"Milk and sugar?"

I nod.

Ford hands me a steaming mug. "Help yourself to a bun."

"Thanks."

I'm stuffing cinnamon bun into my face when she says, "I got a call from Ms. Haslett about an hour ago."

I nearly choke.

"She said you went to your last home and let yourself in. Apparently gave Mrs. Kirble quite a scare." Her mouth tightens into the same thin line as Betty's.

"That's a lie!" Suddenly I'm standing, my words exploding. "A stinking lie!"

Ford's mouth opens. She looks as surprised as I am, but I'm not stopping.

I whip the bun into the kitchen sink. "Fuck Betty, fuck Haslett, and fuck you!" I'm out of the kitchen, slamming the front door, and striding down the walk when I feel cold moving up my legs, realize I'm not wearing shoes. Or a coat.

The rage drains out of me fast as it came. I teeter at the edge of the sidewalk and gaze through tears at the slush around my feet.

I hear the front door open. Ford says, "Come inside, before you freeze." She sounds tired.

When I turn around, she's not there, but the door is still open.

Seven

Lunch on Monday, I head to the edge of the forest again telling myself that somehow I'll make friends at this school, but the cafeteria crowd seems too clannish to waste my effort on.

Sitting on a boulder beneath the bough of a pine tree, I pull my peanut butter sandwich out of my lunch bag and discover a tinfoil package Ford must have sneaked in. Feels like cookies.

Five — no, six — chocolate-chip cookies. They smell intense. I crunch into one of them and hit a ton of creamy dark chocolate.

A memory pops then fizzles like fireworks. Still, it leaves me smiling: Dad holding a tray of cookies, grinning as he says, "Dig in, Sebastian!"

Ford's surprise gift makes three foster-family firsts. And Sunday morning when we talked, she never lost it. After I said, *Sorry,* and told her what really happened, she said a bunch of stuff like, *We both deserve common courtesy . . . We'll have to work on trusting each other.* When she said, *Sometimes it feels as though life's good things don't last long enough,* I did a double take — almost asked her why *she* said that.

Maybe she really is different, like Hassles said. Hope she's not like Betty — putting on a show till it doesn't suit her anymore.

She gave me more milk money, but said she'll pick up my new clothes to save time. As if. Second-hand, here we come. Least she doesn't keep all the CSC money for herself.

Lunch is done — except the cookies, which I've saved for last — when five guys shuffle out of the forest farther from the school than I am. The guy in the lead is big, blond with black roots, almost tall as me, but wider.

He passes a package to a skinny little dude and waits while the dude tucks it into a pocket partway down the leg of his cargo pants and then pulls a black hoodie over his do-rag.

The others go ahead, passing me without a glance.

When the big blond and the little guy are about ten feet away the big one fixes red, skunk-swollen eyes on me.

The little guy's probably got a pocketful of pot. He keeps going, shoulders hunched, head jutting like a vulture. "Let's go, bro."

The big guy doesn't budge. His head tilts to one side as he checks me out.

I put the cookies down and stand. "You want a picture or what?"

"Huh?" He blinks.

I'm about to tell this ape to piss off, when he grins. "Sebastian, man! What the hell?" With three steps, he's in front of me. Who is this guy?

He holds a hand up, shoulder level. "Five up high!"

I give him a high five.

The little dude stops to watch.

The big one holds his hand out by his thigh. "Now, five down low."

Scrambling through my memory, I go to slap his hand again.

He pulls it away. "Oh! Way too slow!"

I haven't done that goofy routine in years.

"What the fuck was that, Don?" the little guy asks.

A name pops into my head. "Donny Malner. Right? Whoa. This is taking me back. Baseball."

Donny nods. "Sebastian Till."

"It's Seb, now."

"I knew I knew that freaky orange hair. You liked playing first base. Hey," he calls to the other guy. "Come here!"

I can only remember a couple things about Donny: he was a grade ahead of me, and the only chubby kid on the team. "You were the kid who always had candy to share, right?"

"That's me." He grins. "Still the candy man. But smarter about which candy I put away." He pats his stomach. No fat now.

"You sure grew."

"You too, man." He laughs. "Good thing that schnozz of yours didn't grow like the rest of you. It's still honkin'!" He can't stop laughing. Must have been some strong pot.

"Guess it's what you'd call *classic* — " Chris' nice word for my nose.

"Yeah." Donny gets a grip. Coughs. "Sorry, man."

I shrug.

He turns to his buddy. "Sean, meet Sebastian, an old pal from back in the day."

Old pal? I nod, stand a little straighter, and hold out my hand to Sean. "Hey. It's Seb, now."

Sean grunts, then — ignoring my hand — tucks a few strands of straight brown hair under his do-rag. "We gotta bounce, Don."

I stuff my hands in my pockets.

"Relax, man! So, Sebastian, what are you doing here?"

"Oh, I've been moving around since . . . " Suddenly, my chest feels like it's in a Vise-Grip.

"Oh yeah." Donny looks at Sean. "Sebastian's parents bought it in a car crash. When you were, what . . . seven, eight?"

"Uh-huh." I try to breathe deep without it showing.

"That's rough." Donny shakes his head.

Sean's expression doesn't change. "Too bad. I guess. Wish I were so lucky."

My jaw stiffens.

Donny grimaces. "Smooth, asshole."

Sean flips him the finger. "Nothing personal." He shrugs. "Let's go."

"See you around, Sebastian."

They don't seem real tight. *Old pal.* They've only gone a couple steps when I call, "Hey, Donny? Don?" That comes out a little too high.

He looks back.

I cut the needy whine. "You wanna get together some time?"

"I guess." He scratches his chin. "Yeah, sure. We can cruise some chicks in my Shelby. You down with that, Sebastian?"

"I sure am, Don."

"Okay. I'll catch you later."

"Later, man."

I finish Ford's cookies, barely believing my good luck.

Over the next week, I spend lunchtimes scanning the forest, roaming the halls, and glancing through the cafeteria. No sight of my *old pal*, but I spot Tiff, the gorgeous girl from Geography, hanging with the same guy a discouraging number of times.

Thursday, I see Donny way down a hall. The lunch crunch is on and it's too crowded to catch up, but when he slips through the door closest to the trees I grab my coat and head for the same place we first met. He doesn't show. I down my lunch figuring I'll be in juvie or a group home by the time he comes looking for me — if he ever does.

After lunch, I'm fishing my geography books out of my locker when a girl says, "Hi, Seb."

I spin around, nearly dislocating my shoulder.

Nina — the chick with all the hair who saved me from punching crazy Markus — opens a locker across the hall from mine and shoves in a violin case.

"Hey, Nina. That your locker?"

"Don't tell me you just noticed." She pushes her lips out like an angry duck.

I swallow a laugh. "Sorry."

"That's okay." She shrugs. "Every time I saw you over there, I just assumed you were the silent stalker type."

"Stalker! I — "

"I'm kidding." She winks then grabs some books. "But I have seen you furtively dogging the flight attendant."

"What are you talking about?"

She spins the dial on her lock. "That's nicer than calling her an airhead, don't you think?"

"Who?"

"Tiff."

My ear heats up. "*Dogging? Furtively?* That sounds disgusting."

She laughs. "What do you want to bet she won't be in Geography? She only shows up about twice a month."

"Really? I mean, you're in that class, too?"

"Again? Seriously?" She pats her hair. "You missed *this* in that closet?"

"Sorry. Again." I follow her into Waldozer's room wondering who's the bigger goof — her or me.

Of course, the desk behind mine is empty.

Friday afternoon, I'm plodding through the school parking lot when two girls rush past, one texting, the other saying they've got to make it home from the mall in time to meet *everyone.*

Wish I had anyone. Wish I had something to do besides watch TV with Ford. Mr. Frogley's a great old guy, and I like helping him do the janitor thing. But I've already visited three times this week, after telling Ford I'm going for a jog.

A tricked-out black car blocks my way. The driver — too old for high school — is talking to some guy who's leaning over, arm resting on the roof, head lowered. Before I can detour, the car inches forward and the guy straightens up.

"Hey, Donny!" I remind myself of Maggie squealing *It's Red* and hope the rumble of the car muffled my voice.

Donny looks at me with eyes half-shut, as though he's puzzled, or pissed.

I clear my throat. "That was some sweet ride. Eh, Don?"

He shrugs. "Sebastian. What's doing?"

"Not much."

Suddenly, he smiles. "I just got an excellent idea. You in a rush?"

"No. Not at all."

"I say we go burn before heading home. You into it?"

"Burn? Dope?" Shut up, idiot!

Hassles' warning sounds: I get caught, I'm screwed.

But this could be my only chance to get in with Donny. But — *just say no* . . .

"Geez, Sebastian." Donny knuckle-punches my shoulder. "I thought it was an easy question."

"Yeah! I'm into it." The words fall out before I'm finished thinking.

Eight

As we head for the pine forest, I keep looking around for snitches, even though nobody knows my name or could care less.

"Chill out, Sebastian," Donny says. "You'll make people wonder what we're up to."

Donny's so cool. If he's not worried, why should I be? No way am I telling him I've only ever shared a single joint with four guys.

"So, where've you been since Little League, Sebastian?"

"Moving around." Sounds better than living with a psycho, a drunk, or a bunch of hypocrites.

"What do you mean?"

We duck into the trees and follow a muddy path.

"Living with different foster families."

"Oh? How many?"

"I don't know . . . four?"

"Four?" He sounds surprised. "That's fairly fucked."

I shrug, glad I didn't tell him the truth. "It's pretty typical for a kid old as I was. The first couple happened so fast, I barely remember them."

"No shit?"

I nod.

Donny shakes his head and plunks down in the middle of a log barely twenty feet into the pines. Anyone who tried could probably see us from the street.

There's no room for me to sit, so I just stand there, feeling stuck as a post.

"You know something, Sebastian?" He pulls a tobacco pouch from his pants pocket. "You remind me of your dad."

"You remember him?" I step closer, force myself to stay cool. "Really?"

"Sure. You look like him, except for your hair. He used to come out to our games."

"Yeah? I forgot that." My whole body is vibrating with excitement. I haven't met anyone who knew Dad before . . .

"Yeah." Donny picks a couple of rolling papers from the pouch. "He always knew my name. I liked that." He tears one of the papers in half then licks and sticks it to the longer one. "Shit. Your old man knew everybody's name. Maybe because he was always scorekeeper."

"Yeah!" I can see Dad standing behind a batter's cage, clipboard in hand. Donny pulls some weed from the pouch. The skunky smell mixes with soggy forest scent, sparking a memory of the little shitter I ate with in the back room at foster home three.

"I didn't really understand," Donny says, "but your dad was always talking numbers — the *stats*."

"Oh yeah!" Focus on the good stuff, Seb. "I forgot that, too." That why I'm good with numbers?

"I've got a good memory." Donny mixes some tobacco into the weed in his palm. "In fact — no offence, man — but, weren't you a bit of a nerd back then? You know, a little *yes-man*." His voice goes way high. "*Whatever-you-say, daddy?*"

I force a smile. "If I was, it sure didn't help me."

"Hmm?"

"I mean, I didn't get adopted." My jaw tenses. "I never even got invited to eat with one of my lousy foster families."

"Huh?" He gives the joint a lick and a twist. "So, what have you been up to, besides working on your table manners?"

I scramble to prove I'm not a lame goody-goody. "Actually, I just got busted a couple months ago."

"Oh?" He looks up, interested, then pulls a lighter from his pocket and fires up the joint.

Dad and Mom's faces flash through my brain. What am I doing? I want to take back my words, but — "That's why I'm here now."

"Really, eh?" He inhales deeply, watching me.

"Yeah. I get bounced every time I get in trouble." True, but . . .

He nods, then after holding the smoke in his lungs forever, exhales. "So, looks like you've changed."

"I guess so." I glance out towards the street. Wish we'd get back to Dad.

"Have a seat, Sebastian." He slides over, hands me the joint. "Why'd you — ?"

"Hey, Donny," I say, hoping to stop his questions. "Remember that funny guy on the team? Guy with the big teeth?" I take a toke.

"Glenn!" Donny laughs.

My act gets slightly shredded when I cough. I try to cover, saying, "This is some good stuff." As if I have a clue. "Yeah — Glenn."

Donny takes the joint. "That kid was hilarious! "Remember that practice when home plate was a giant mud puddle?"

I frown.

"Sure you do. Coach told us to stay away, but Glenn edged halfway around it holding onto the inside of the backstop, and then — " Donny cracks up.

"Oh yeah!" Suddenly I picture Glenn, one hand gripping the wire mesh, the other waving as he calls over his shoulder, *Look guys! I'm Spider-Man.*

I laugh. "Then he fell spread-eagle on his back in the mud."

Donny nods and passes the joint to me. "Or that time he dove for home and lost his pants?" He chuckles.

As Donny comes up with a story for just about every kid on our old team, the joint slides back and forth. When it's done, he rolls another and says, "You know those ass-wipes who didn't let you eat with them? Maybe they thought being an orphan was a disease their real kids could catch. Eh, Sebastian?" He laughs.

"Maybe." I shrug.

We smoke and talk, and it's like we're old friends. It's almost too easy. But — I guess we really *are* old friends!

While Donny rolls a third doobie, I gaze at the pine needles on a branch beside me. "They're amazing, eh? Like perfect little green bicycle spokes."

Donny laughs. "Sure." He takes the roach and lights the new one with it. After exhaling he says, "This stuff is kind of weak, eh?"

"Oh?" I nod then steady myself to keep from falling off the log.

Donny laughs again. "So, not including falling over, what sort of trouble have you been getting into?"

"Well, the latest was larceny." The lawyer's word. I laugh. "Sounds like I burned something down — right?"

Donny shrugs. "I never thought of that. What did you steal?"

"Me and a buddy liberated some stuff to help do a B and E."

"Really?" He sounds impressed. "So, what happened?"

"We got caught breaking into a building full of stuff we were going to sell."

"You're kidding?"

"I'm not." Am I?

After we kill the joint, Donny says, "I'm going to a party tonight, Sebastian. Want to come? There should be lots of hot chicks."

"Sure!" I feel like Skinny leaping for food.

"Come to my place first. 10 Chestnut Grove." He pulls a pen from his jacket pocket. "Write that down. And lose the dumb grin. It could get you in trouble."

My ear heats up. I scribble his address on my hand.

He glances at it. "Good. Seven thirty, eight okay?"

"No problem." The top of my head feels like it could lift off.

I start for home feeling light, like a weight's been dropped. I haven't spent a second worrying about court or anything since we finished the second doobie. And I'm not thinking about much except hot chicks, food, and how they get the sidewalk lines so straight and perfectly spaced, when a cop car slides by. It slows.

K.J. Rankin

A cop gives me a laser-like stare. Can he tell I'm stoned?

Suddenly my eyes feel dry and itchy. A voice in my head screams, *Run!*

I try to act normal, look back down at the sidewalk. What was so interesting a couple seconds ago? Should I pretend I dropped something? Smile at the officer? Whistle? I force my feet to keep moving, tell them to hold the beat so we don't get busted.

Finally, the cops pull away. Even after they make a turn and disappear, my legs feel skittery, like they might fly out from under me.

So much for not worrying.

I'm still a wreck when Skinny shows up a few blocks from Ford's. So, instead of heading straight home, I wander through the neighbourhood with Skinny for another hour or so, until most of me stops buzzing.

At Ford's I call, "Hi. Stayed late to work on a project," and head straight for my room where I stash my jacket in the closet in case it stinks. Next, I wash up as well as I can without getting into the shower. After that, I sit, stunned, a book propped open in front of me, until Ford calls me for dinner.

Nine

By 7:30 PM, I've made it through dinner, pocketed some of it for the mutt, and almost finished drying the dishes, as usual, without Ford noticing anything except that I love her food. And I've decided that if Donny breaks out the weed tonight, I'm passing. I don't need to get scared legless again.

Ford's at the table, folding clean napkins. "I don't usually have such a willing helper. I really appreciate it, Seb."

She stops folding and runs a thumb back and forth over the big knuckle of her other thumb. She does that a fair bit but she's nothing like Grumpy-Gram who didn't do much but complain, which would get 'Aunty' yelling at 'Uncle.' *You decide! Who's leaving? Me? Or your mother?* I wished he'd say, *Both of you.* I point at Ford's hand. "I knew a lady who wore a band like that, only on her wrist, for her arthritis."

"Oh!" She continues folding. "Interesting."

After putting away the last pot, I go grab my coat and call, "See you later!"

She pops into the hall. "Where are you off to, Seb?"

I don't really know doesn't seem like a good answer.

"You haven't forgotten the deal we made after your last excursion, have you?" She's not smiling. "If you want to go out for the evening, I need to know where."

Psycho-Dad bursts into my brain. *I need to know, you lying little shit.* The belt coming off.

"So, you don't trust me? I didn't lie."

"Please tone it down, Seb." She isn't shouting. "I didn't say you had lied." She isn't losing it, either. "That's not the issue. It's just part of being courteous, to say nothing of my CSC responsibilities."

I try to shake Psycho-Dad. "I got invited to a party."

"Okay. Where is it?"

"At Donny's place." It's not, but . . .

"Donny who? Where does he live?"

"Malner." I hand her the scrap of paper I've copied his address to.

"Thank you. Will his parents be home?"

I shrug. "Far as I know."

"Hmm." She pulls her glasses from her apron pocket. "This is literally 'on the other side of the tracks,' Seb. Do you know how to get there?"

"Figure I'll find my way."

"It's a good forty, fifty-minute walk — unless you get lucky with the buses which, at this time of day isn't likely. I'll draw a map, just in case." She sits down at the phone table and grabs a pencil.

I drum my fingers on the living room door frame, hoping to speed her up.

Finally she hands Donny's address back. "We're here." She points at her map. "And he's approximately there." Next she takes a couple of bus tokens from a drawer in the table and hands them over with a small shrug. "You never know. Nevertheless, I expect you to be home by eleven. Is that clear?"

That's ridiculous, but I gotta get going. "Clear."

At the bottom of the driveway, Skinny wolfs down his bit of dinner then follows me all the way to Donny's.

Ford's living room would fit into Donny's front hall. A stairway leads up to the second floor. As I follow Donny toward another set of stairs going down, I tilt my head back, look up two whole storeys to the ceiling, and feel even taller — like a giant in his castle.

"My old lady's home with a headache, so we're keeping it quiet," Donny says, trotting down to the basement.

Sean taps the buttons on one of two old-fashioned pinball machines near the stairs. Guess Donny and him are tighter than I thought. His pants hang so low, they remind me of Little J with a loaded diaper. He nods at me without stopping his game. Red, white, and yellow lights flash as the metal ball bounces from one corner of the board to the other.

Donny's place has everything. On the far side of the room, a huge screen faces three rows of fat, black, leather chairs and little tables. Behind those, there's a red-roofed glass hut on wheels, with a mountain of popcorn inside. A counter runs along part of the back wall with cupboards full of glasses stretching up to the ceiling, and more cupboards hiding who-knows-what under it.

"Awesome set-up, Don."

"Yeah, Don," Sarcasm creeps into Sean's voice. "You the shiz."

Donny smiles. "Want to play pinball, Sebastian?"

61

"I never tried."

"So, go for it!" He points to a dish of coins. "Slugs for the machines."

"Cool!"

"I'll be back down in a bit."

"Okay. But, we don't want to be late for the party, Don," I call.

He bounds up the stairs without answering.

Sean snorts. "You a girl, or what?"

I feel like saying, *You fill your diaper, or what?* "It's just, Donny — Don — said there'd be some hot chicks." I'm sure as hell not mentioning my stupid curfew.

"True." Sean smacks a button and the silver ball careens into a bumper. "But we'll get there. Meantime, watch and learn from the master." He makes the little ball roll up and down a flipper. "You gotta slow it down, man. *Finesse* the shot." He pops the ball up. It hits a target, rolls through a spinner thing, then drops into a hole. The lights and points-counter go crazy. He grins.

We play till I've used up most of the slugs and Sean's said, "Who da master?" about a thousand times.

Finally, I say, "What's Don doing up there?"

Sean starts another ball. "Getting his shit together for Crystal's."

I figure that means he's rolling a lot of joints.

Donny calls down the stairs, "Okay, boys. Time to bounce."

"We taking the wheels?" Sean asks.

"Walking. Crystal's place isn't far."

Sean groans. "I *hate* walkin'. You *not* the shiz, Don."

Donny laughs. "You could try pulling up your pants, goof."

Sean frowns. "Watch it, bro. Don't be calling me *goof*."

We've gone a couple of blocks when Sean says, "That dog's following us."

I look back. Sure enough, Skinny's keeping his distance, but he's following.

Sean hitches up his pants, walks faster. "Maybe got rabies."

"It's okay," I say. "He's cool."

⌣

Crystal's place is like Donny's, only on steroids. Before we head up the walk, Donny pulls out his phone and texts someone. "Just letting her know we're here."

"I guess everyone here will be from your grade?" I say, wondering if I'll see Tiff.

Donny snorts. "This is a private-school crowd."

"Then, why are *we* here?"

"Oh, yeah," Sean says. "Almost forgot." He pulls a huge gold dollar symbol from under his hoodie so it hangs down his chest.

Donny shakes his head. "Real subtle."

Sean shrugs. "The chicks love it."

Donny pushes the bell and a second later the super-sized front door opens. Pop music spills out and a blonde in glitzy gold grabs Donny's jacket with one hand and Sean's hoodie with the other. She gives them each a quick kiss, then peers at me.

Donny says, "I brought a friend. Cool?"

She flashes a smile. "I'm Crystal."

I nod. "Seb."

"Come on in." She steps back. "You guys are just what this party needs."

No kiss for me.

Across the massive front hall, a bunch of girls sit on wide stairs that wind up to a second-floor balcony-type landing. They're gabbing at top volume over the music and only a few glance our way.

Crystal says something to Donny. He pulls a small tinfoil package from a pocket and hands it to her.

She shoves it into the waistband of her skin-tight pants. As the music fades, she says, "I'll get you later, Don."

Donny nods.

Guess he's got more than weed going on.

"Absolutely no smoking in the house, you guys. Okay?" Crystal waits for me to nod.

She flashes another smile then hurries away as reggae floods the air. Halfway down the front hall, she yells back at Donny. "Be careful, eh? I'll catch total shit if the cops show again."

Cops? Here? No way. I sure hope not.

"Let's go find some drinks." Donny's voice is nearly drowned by The Wailers'.

The music vibrates through my body as I follow Donny and Sean into a room packed with people dancing and lit by a dim glow around the edge of the ceiling. It smells like sweat and . . . what?

Booze.

Dad-A-Dick looms in my thoughts, sending prickles over my scalp. I hold my breath and shove him out of my brain.

Sean drops onto a low couch between a couple making out and some guy who smiles and thumps him on the back. Weaving past dancers, I follow Donny, deaf to whatever he shouts over his shoulder every so often.

He wasn't kidding about there being a lot of hot chicks. There's got to be two girls for every guy. In the kitchen, the few guys hanging around don't pay any attention when Donny helps himself to a couple beers from a cooler. He shoves one at me like it's no big deal, so I put on my poker face and mumble, "Thanks." I can handle a few beers no problem.

"I'm going upstairs for a bit," he shouts. "You hang down here, Sebastian. Don't do anything I wouldn't do." He knuckle-punches my shoulder then goes through an open door at the back of the kitchen and up a narrow staircase. A couple of the guys head up the stairs behind him.

Chris managed to lift some of his brother's beer for us once in a while — closest I ever got to partying. I down mine in a few quick gulps, picturing Chris and me hiding behind the furnace in his basement, chugging in case we got caught.

Sean saunters into the kitchen with two red-eyed girls in tow, nods at me, grabs a few beers, and then wanders back out.

Since nobody seems to care, I take another beer, impressed by how smoothly I've slid into this party scene.

Leaning against the living-room wall, my legs strategically crossed, I sip beer not far from a huddle of dancing, talking, laughing girls. I nod in time to the rap, hope I look cool — not like some spineless giraffe. I've never seen so many gorgeous girls.

Would any of them say *yes* if I asked her to dance?

Can I dance?

After about thirty minutes, I've finished my beer and still haven't found the guts to go near the girls. I feel like a hopeless wall-weed. I'm about to go look for Donny and Sean when a pink-haired chick in a sizzling chrome-coloured dress breaks from the pack and walks in my direction.

She's looking at me, but probably headed for the kitchen. Anyhow, she's not that pretty and way too short for me.

She stops in front of me, stares up with beautiful green eyes, and smiles.

My legs go soft.

Ten

Her kissable pink lips say something I can't hear. I bend forward, wondering if she needs me to reach something down for her.

Water bottle in hand, she stretches an arm up, hooks it around my neck, and then tugs.

"Whoa!" I jerk back a little to keep my balance. Mumble, "Sorry."

As I'm pulled lower, more of her bare arm wraps around my neck, sending a shiver down my spine. She smells like honey.

I spy a lacy bit of bra just past the edge of her top. My heart goes into overdrive.

"What's up?" I ask, glad she can't hear my nerves rattling.

Her lips are so close to my ear I can feel her breath. "Hey, big guy," she says, rubbing my shoulder. "You want me to rock your world?"

The empty beer can slips from my hand. I choke out, "Yes." Before I can say anything else, she lets go of my shoulder, grabs my hand, and pulls me into the crowd of dancers. She looks sexy just taking a sip of water. I can't believe my luck. I'm in love. "What's your name?"

I figure she can't hear me, but then she looks back, eyes sparkling. "Rose."

Rose. Beautiful Rose.

Another chick steps in front of her, as if to block her way. She's frowning, shouting something that's lost in the tunes. Rose hands her the water. The other one shakes her head, still pissed off, and turns away.

Rose pulls me over to a corner of the room, far from the group of girls she was with. If she wants to disappear, it won't happen with me. But I'd drop to my knees, do anything, for her.

She takes both my hands in hers, stands with her back to me, and moves to the beat, her whole body doing this sexy side-to-side thing. My pants get tighter.

A slow song starts. She turns around, grabs my belt and pulls me close.

My hands wrap around her, feel her warmth through her thin top. I pull back. Don't want my hard-on freaking her out. She stretches a hand up to my neck and pulls my head down again.

I think geography, math, anything to stop me exploding. But we don't kiss. She breathes into my ear again. "I'm so hot. Am I making you crazy, too?"

"Yes!" I nod, my heart — everything — ready to blast off.

Three squared, nine, four squared, sixteen, five squared, twenty-five . . .

"Come on." Her hand clamps on my belt and she pulls me through the crush of bodies.

I can't believe it! "Where are we going?"

No answer. I can't blow this.

Seven squared, forty-nine. Eight squared, sixty . . .

Sean, standing with some other guys, slides past. He nods at me and moves his hand in the air like he's beating off.

Goof.

Rose leads me through the kitchen to the same door Donny used. Next she's floating backwards up the stairs, her fingers saying follow me. I take one step up, another, and then another. She's three steps higher and our heads are almost level. The music thunders.

She leans toward me. Our lips touch and then her tongue is moving around mine. I can barely keep myself from coming.

She turns away so fast my tongue's left sticking out for a moment. Fuckin' embarrassing. Following her gaze, I look up the stairs.

A guy the size of a lineman is charging down.

She moves to let him pass.

He doesn't. Wedged in beside her, he shoves her up a couple more steps.

I grab his arm. "Don't you touch her!"

His foot catches me in the chest. I lose my hold, fall backwards, whack my head against the door frame, and then crumple onto the floor.

As the music and my boner die, Rose yells, "What the hell's wrong with you, Ryan?"

I'm in too much pain to do anything but blink up at them, wondering if I'll be able to move before the lineman — Ryan — finishes me off.

Rose pushes the guy's hand off her waist and says, "You don't own me."

I manage to gasp, "Yeah. She's with me."

Ryan shakes his head and sighs. "You're out of control, Kiera."

Kiera?

"How many times do I have to tell you?" Ryan sounds almost bored. "You don't need X, babe. You got it all going on without that shit. And look what you did to that poor boy."

"What I did?" Rose — Kiera? — shrieks, then giggles.

My heart stops. "What the hell?" comes out like a whisper.

The music blares again. Rose — whoever — peers down at me. She blows me a kiss, says something to Ryan, and then she kisses him. The same way she kissed me.

"What the hell?" I shout, but neither of them even looks my way.

They climb the stairs holding hands.

X? She took ecstasy? That's the only reason she wanted me?

I want to puke, kill somebody. Most of all, I want to disappear.

Donny leans over me, frowning. He says something then reaches down. I let him pull me up so I'm sitting on my aching butt, then I stumble to my feet.

He hands me another beer. "You wasted?"

"No." I touch the lump growing on the back of my head. "But, I'm done here."

Donny scans the dark street. "Too bad I didn't bring the wheels. I could've given you a lift home."

I try not to tremble. "I'm okay with walking." We're standing beneath a street lamp in front of Crystal's place. It's a relief not to have to shout. Shouting hurts my head.

Donny pulls out his cell phone. "I'll call you a taxi."

"I want to walk." More like crawl. "With my bruised ass, I won't be sitting for a while." I force a smile.

"I can pay."

I take my last gulp of beer. "Really, man. Walking."

Music blares from the front door. Sean saunters down the porch steps and across the lawn. "Yo, Don! What you doing out here? There's lots more biz in there, bro."

Donny stares at Sean for a long moment, then turns to me. "You sure you're okay?"

"Yeah." I toss the empty can onto the grass. I'm tempted to ask, *What's the biz?* But I'm pretty sure I already know, and I don't feel like being lied to anymore tonight.

Sean stops beside us. "'Sup?"

"Kier and Ryan did their gong-show on Sebastian."

Sean smirks. "Sucks to be you. Can't say I didn't warn you about that chick."

"Huh? The weird wave was supposed to be a warning?"

"Yeah." Sean nods slowly, like he's some real wise guy. "I gave you the DIY sign. That chick is fucked in the head, bro."

Donny chuckles. "Sean's just pissed 'cause Kiera doesn't like little guys."

"Hey!" Sean's jaw juts out. "You calling me *little*? 'Cause that is *not* the case, bro." He grabs his crotch and grins. "Her eyes would'a popped if she'd seen what I got."

Donny laughs. "That chick *is* messed. Don't let it get to you, Sebastian."

"Private school," Sean mutters.

Donny shrugs. "She likes to get Ryan going."

Sean nods. "And X makes her super horny."

"Oh yeah?" I'm ninety-nine percent sure who supplied the X.

Donny fakes a cough.

Sean's eyebrows slide up to the edge of his do-rag. "She always goes for that. Speaking of which, we gotta get back in there, Don."

Donny frowns.

Sean spreads his hands. "I mean — there's lots of babes just waiting for us, bro."

Donny glances at his phone. "Okay. Catch you later, Sebastian."

As I slog home along quiet streets, a million thoughts grind through my brain. Did she really want me? Was it just the X? Why the phony name? If Ryan hadn't shown, would I be doing it with her now? I'm not sure of anything, except that Donny and Sean are dealers.

And, really, I couldn't care less about their business . . . long as I stay out of it. Donny's a good guy.

A few blocks from home, Skinny shows up.

"Hey!" I give him a pat. "Where'd you come from?"

He trots ahead, looking back every so often as though he's worried about me. At Ford's, I give him a good rub. "Wish I could invite you in, boy." He licks my hand then watches me slip through the front door.

Ford pads out of her bedroom, book in hand and wearing a dressing gown and slippers. "I knew you'd make it home by eleven. You're actually a little early. Did you have a good time?"

"I guess." I'd forgotten all about my stupid curfew. "But I'm tired."

"So am I." She takes off her glasses. "Time to stop reading. Good night, Seb. Sweet dreams."

"Yeah. Sure." I touch the bump on the back of my head and then plod down the hall to my room.

Eleven

The following week, I'm at my locker grabbing some books and imagining for the millionth time what might have happened if Ryan hadn't come down those stairs. At least it's better than wondering what'll happen in court, which was practically all I thought about before last Friday.

"Hey, Seb!" Nina strides along the hall, her hair a bouncy mess of tight curls. "Pretty impressive performance in math. I could use your help."

I shrug. "Sure." Math is about the only thing that always comes easy at school.

"Have you started your glacier report?" she asks.

"Huh?"

"Hold on. I bet I look like an overgrown Chia Pet." She opens her locker and half of her disappears into it. After some thumps and a 'damn it,' she backs out wearing a band over her hair that says, *Four legs good. Two legs bad.* "Are you laughing at me?"

I swallow my smile. "No."

"So, about glaciers. You know — brief class presentation?"

Maybe nailing that door frame affected my memory. "Sounds familiar," I lie and rub the back of my head — lump's finally gone.

"Since we both got glaciers, I think we should coordinate our presentations today or tomorrow so that we don't bore everyone."

"I'm bored already. When's it due?"

She sighs. "Two weeks from Thursday."

"Seriously?" No wonder I forgot about it.

Her eyes narrow. "You haven't even started, have you?"

"Course I have." Another lie.

"I bet." She winks.

"Let's figure out who says what in a couple weeks. Okay, Nina?"

"That's pushing it." She closes her locker. "But, at least you'll be ready by then."

"I guess." With court coming first, I may not even be here by then.

At lunch time, I'm peering down a locker-lined hall looking for Donny when Nina shows up with some short, plump guy. "Seb, this is Matt. He's in Geography too, in case you never noticed." She winks. Really likes winking.

"You're coming to the caf with us, Seb?" Matt asks.

Right. We'll be the lunch bunch of losers.

"Yes, he is." Nina says as though I've already agreed. "Come on." She heads down the hall. "I'm starving and I forgot my lunch."

Matt shrugs. His crooked smile seems to say, *Gotta go with it.*

No sign of Donny since Friday. Lunch with these two just might be better than eating alone again. Matt hurries to catch up with Nina.

I hang behind. The few stragglers who haven't already settled somewhere rush past.

"You don't have to walk three steps back, Seb," Nina calls without stopping. "Even though I've been told I resemble some amazing Greek goddess."

Matt snorts. "Yeah, right. Would that be Medusa?"

Two girls passing by giggle.

Nina stops and points at Matt. "Silence, mortal. Medusa was not a goddess, and you're just envious." She stalks away.

"Envious?" Matt almost trips over his own feet trying to keep pace with her.

"Admit it, Matt. You've always wanted big hair."

"Oh, yeah." He looks back at me, grins. "And small boobs."

Nina shrugs. "You said it, Matt. Not me."

"Ouch."

I don't know Medusa, but these guys are good for a laugh.

I follow Matt and Nina to an empty table. Unwrapping my sandwich, I'm almost as pumped as I was when I found Ford's stash of roast beef this morning. I forgot about court, even Rose, while I slapped my sandwich together.

Matt flips through a magazine, picks at a bag of chips, and sucks on his can of Diet Coke; Nina ploughs steadily through her lunch, starting with a cheeseburger and fries.

I gaze around the cafeteria, looking for Donny.

Matt says, "Do you play anything, Seb?"

"Poker, once in a while."

"I meant an instrument."

Nina pauses before inhaling half a cupcake. "Matt's a drummer."

"Oh?" Hard to imagine.

As Nina talks about Matt's band, Tiff floats through the cafeteria. I picture her pulling me close, saying the words playing in my head since Friday: *I'm so hot. You want me to rock your world?*

Nina peers over her shoulder, then back at me. Through a mouthful of icing, she says, "Forget about it. She's practically married."

I try to look puzzled. "What're you talking about?"

Matt closes the magazine. "Mind your own business, Nina."

"You can't fool me, Seb. I heard that big sigh."

"Give him a break."

"I'm just trying to give him a clue, because . . . " She licks a finger clean then waves at someone behind me. "Because he's new here. Plus . . . " She whispers. "I can tell you're terribly shy — just like me." Another wink.

"Maybe Nina's got the hots for you, Seb."

There goes the ear. I gulp my milk.

Nina glares at Matt. "Actually, I'm waiting for a man with more facial hair than I have."

A mouthful of milk nearly squirts out my nose.

Nina leans across the table, whispers loudly, "We Greek girls are constantly plucking and shaving."

Wiping water from my eyes, I check her out. Other than her intense eyebrows, I don't see any outgrowth.

Matt snorts. "Some goddess. You're grossing out the new guy."

"No way! He's got a sense of humour."

"So, that *plucking and shaving* was a joke?" I ask.

She shrugs. "But don't be offended by my facial hair comment. When you gagged — just now? I couldn't help noticing your very manly Adam's apple." She smiles before gulping her chocolate milk.

"I knew it," Matt says. "You're a sap for other stick people."

"You could turn that into a syrupy love song." Nina pats Matt's hand. "And don't worry, Matty. Remember, opposites attract."

"Are you implying that I'm fat, or gorgeous?"

On my way out of the cafeteria, I realize that I haven't worried about anything for almost an hour.

I don't see Donny until the next day, after my second lunch with Nina and Matt. I'm on my way to Math when he appears out of nowhere.

"Sebastian! You're a hard guy to find."

"Donny! Don. I've been looking for you, too, man."

"I've just got a second. Are you going this way?"

I nod and turn around.

"I'm getting a few folks together this Saturday," he says. "You up for some action?"

"Sure! What sort of action?" Striding shoulder to shoulder along the hall, I picture Donny and me surrounded by a flock of beautiful girls.

Donny tilts his head. "You never know."

"Will Kiera be there?"

"No worries — none of those chicks. Show up around nine."

"That's kind of late," I say, remembering Ford's last curfew.

"We have to wait for my parents to disappear." He shrugs then stops and grabs a closing classroom door. "Cool, Sebastian?"

"Cool!" I speed to Math hoping that door won't be closed, and wondering if Ford will give me an extra hour or two.

⌇

"Seb, I don't suppose you have any interest in gardening?" Ford gazes out the kitchen window as she fills the sink to wash our Saturday brunch dishes.

I manage to catch *No* before it slips out. "Gardening?" None of my other foster parents have done that.

"Because I could use some help."

"I don't mind helping," I say hopefully, curfew in mind.

"Wonderful!" She dumps cutlery into the soapy water. "That back fence looks too bare with the old maple gone."

"Oh?"

"I finally lost it to the gypsy moths last year."

"I've heard of gypsies," I say, clearing the table. "But gypsy moths?"

"Their larvae strip the leaves off hardwoods. Anyhow, I'd like to make a new flower bed there."

"What do you want me to do? Dig up the grass? I could go do that right after the dishes." I grab a towel to dry. "How big do you want it?"

She chuckles. "I like your enthusiasm. Spring is coming early this year. Who knows? We may be able to start next weekend."

Work next week won't help me with tonight's curfew, but I figure there won't be any better time to ask. "You know the guy who invited me to a party last week?"

"Donny Malner on Chestnut Grove." She puts the clean cutlery in the drainer.

"Well, he invited me over again tonight." I'm sticking to the truth this time.

"Oh! Are you the only one he's invited, or will there be others?" She washes and I dry as we talk.

"There'll just be a few people."

She looks me in the eye. "Will his parents be home, Seb?"

"Donny said to come at nine because he's waiting for them."

She doesn't ask *to come?* or *to leave?* "All right. But I want you home by eleven, again." She piles the dishes in the sink.

"Eleven!" I try to sound surprised. "I'm not getting there till late, and he lives so far away."

"There's no need to raise your voice."

I swallow. "I'm sixteen! You don't have to treat me like a kid."

"I'm well aware that you're sixteen. I'm treating you with respect and setting limits I consider suitable at this point in time." She pats her hands dry on her apron.

"Everyone else will get to stay later." This is hopeless.

"I'll tell you what. Since you were home early last week, you may stay out until eleven thirty this evening. Do we have a deal?"

"How about twelve?"

"Eleven thirty."

I sigh. "Okay."

After dinner, I sneak some leftover brisket into a baggie in my pants pocket. I'm closing the fridge door just as Ford comes back into the kitchen.

I freeze. Did she hear me stealing? Or catch what's missing with *waiting for his parents?*

"I can't believe it!" She opens the cupboard beside the fridge. "I forgot. I made chocolate-chip cookies yesterday, with you in mind."

I start breathing again.

"That last batch disappeared as if by magic," she says.

"They were amazing." The cookies remind me of Ford's lunch-bag surprise, my explosion, Betty's lies.

Ford pries the lid off the cookie tin. "Help yourself."

As I take a few, she smiles. "Enjoy!" Even the wrinkles around her eyes seem to smile.

A while later, I'm tying my shoe laces when she says, "Have a nice time, Seb. I'll see you at eleven thirty."

I look up, ready to give my deadline one last try, but there's that smile again. I'm not exactly sure what it means. But at least it's real. "Yeah. See you."

A block from Ford's place, I toss Skinny the brisket. "Quit looking guilty. Enjoy."

Twelve

"You're the first here." Donny closes the door. As we head down to the basement, he says, "Lucky you didn't come any earlier. My parents only left a few minutes ago."

"Cool. I love your place. Did you live here when we played ball?" I'm hoping he'll say something about Dad.

He nods. "You can play pinball while I put on some tunes and get us a drink."

Seconds later, heavy metal pumps through ceiling speakers, and Donny calls, "Coke?" from the back of the room.

I feed a slug into Jackpot. "Got beer?" Just joking . . . but, you never know.

"No beer."

"Coke's cool." I pull the spring-loaded handle and start a ball rolling. "I wanna get good at this."

"Just aim for the bumpers and keep the ball up."

"Ya — *da master* showed me some tricks."

My second ball drops into the gutter when Donny hands over my Coke. He's wearing some flashy rings I didn't notice before. Weird.

"You like my gear?" He holds up his fist.

"I guess. So . . . you wanna be, like, a gangsta rapper or something?"

"No!" He frowns. "I don't want to be like a fuckin' *gangsta' rapper.* Just rumble-ready."

I laugh. "What? You invited trouble tonight?"

"No, I didn't." He's not laughing. "But I like to be prepared, just in case."

It feels like a pebble just dropped through my gut.

Donny knuckle-punches my shoulder. "No worries, Sebastian."

I chug half my pop. It sizzles down like no other. "What's in this?" I ask, but I already know. Beer's pretty sour, but this stuff adds a sharp almost sweet edge to the Coke. I know the stink of rum. Dad-A-Dick always got hammered on rum, and then hammered anyone who was too slow getting out of his way — usually 'Mom,' sometimes me. I take another swallow remembering how it sucked big-time getting yanked out of there without a chance to say bye to anyone when CSC finally clued in. I swore then I'd never be a drunk.

No, it's not rum. "Vodka?" I gulp some more.

"Scotch. The dickhead counts beer bottles, but since he and Mom both drink scotch, they never know who's running it down." He takes my glass. "I'll get you another."

"Thanks, man. Decent." I can handle it.

"No problem, old buddy."

Old buddy. Donny's gotta be the best thing that's happened to me in ages.

I'm playing Jackpot and working on my second drink when the doorbell sounds faintly against the music.

Donny says, "I'll be right back."

He climbs the stairs four at a time. Must be girls!

I take a swallow of scotch and Coke, gaze around Donny's mind-bending basement, then launch a ball. *Ding, ding, ding.* All right! 300 off the top. I picture a bunch of tall, hot babes slinking down the steps, Crystal saying, *Ladies, meet Sebastian Till: sophisticated yet rugged, red-haired millionaire, a.k.a North America's most sought-after player.* Yeah. Flipper shot — *ding, ding* — another 400.

I gotta calm down. Focus on Jackpot. Look like a pro when the chicks come down. I slap the right flipper. *Ding, ding, ding!* Oh, yeah. *Who da master* now?

Donny thumps back down the stairs with Sean and two other guys. No girls. "Boys, meet Sebastian."

"It's just Seb."

One of the guys is the crazy little dude Nina said to avoid.

Sean glances at my score. "Lame."

I miss a shot. The ball dribbles into the gutter. North America's most desirable player evaporates.

Donny points at the guy to his right. "Geoff."

"Hey, Seb." Geoff smiles, perfect teeth sparkling against brown skin.

"And this is Markus." Donny nods then heads for the fridge.

Markus examines the back of his hands and doesn't even look up. Maybe he won't remember me.

Geoff tilts his head, lowers a shoulder. "Seb, you're so tall, I bet you can't even reach your own toes."

I shrug. "Heard it before."

"Oops!" He slaps a hand over his mouth, makes a face that's so stupid Sean and I laugh. "Okay, no more tall jokes. Besides, I gotta work on my redhead routine."

"Not funny, Geoff." Sean smooths his do-rag, pulls up the hood of his sweatshirt.

Geoff snorts. "Man, you got some serious wanna-be issues."

Markus — still fascinated by his hands — ignores us.

"Don't flatter yourself, Geoff." Sean hikes up his ultra-baggy pants. "I sure don't *wanna be* you."

"That's good, 'cause you ain't got a hope of looking this fine."

Sean farts. "That's what I think of you, Mr. GQ."

Geoff laughs. "Tough guy! You'll never even *smell* as sweet as this stylin' athlete."

Downing some more of my drink, I check out Markus again. He's standing straight as a post now, his eyes fixed like pinpoint lasers on me.

"Don't I know you from somewhere?" he asks.

I shrug.

Donny walks up, drinks in hand. "Sebastian's new around here, Markus."

Markus pushes his chin forward. "I've got the distinct impression you're an ass-wipe."

I point at him. "And you're . . . "

"Already amped." Geoff says. "Best to let it go, Seb." He waves a hand in front of Markus' face. "Down, boy! Anybody ever tell you that too much blow makes you paranoid?"

And — Chris said — makes you think bugs are under your skin. Bet that's why Markus was all over his hands.

"Fuck you." Markus grabs a slug and starts playing Jackpot, throwing ramrod bodychecks at the pinball machine.

"Take it easy, man," Donny says. "It'll tilt."

85

"Tilt?" I ask, as Markus eases up a bit.

"End of game," Donny says. "It shuts down. You boys want a drink?"

"Ya, man," Sean says. "And a bit o' da ganja."

"Fuck off." Donny sounds bored. "He knows we can't smoke in here, Sebastian. My old lady's like a fuckin' hound dog."

I shrug.

Geoff says. "So, are we going cruising this fine evening?"

"You know it." Donny smiles. "Sebastian, want another?"

"Sure."

While Donny gets drinks, Geoff asks how I know him. I tell him about the team. "Little League, or something. All I know is we had a machine spitting out the balls." And all at once I remember Donny having a kicking, screaming fit when his parents forced him into catcher's gear.

Sean starts into a story about sneaking a case of beer into some stadium.

Donny hands me another drink.

The pinball lights blink more brightly. The music seems to fade. Listening to Sean, watching Geoff laugh — I've got this weird feeling, like I'm in a TV commercial or something. Nothing feels too real. I'm not even really real anymore. But it's all good.

I almost told Donny he's the first guy I know with a car — but since nobody else was going ape over his very slick Mustang, I didn't. Now I'm squashed in the back seat between Sean and Geoff. Not sure how that happened. It's not so bad, though. At least my knees — wedged between the bucket seats — are nowhere near Donny's stick shift. Anyway, I'm feeling totally fluid — numb, almost — as I watch the streamers from passing headlights and listen to Geoff's jokes over the tunes.

Beside me, Sean gulps from a flask then passes it. I take a swig, offer it to Geoff. He says, "Let me finish the joke, man. So the pharmacist says, *You idiot! You can't treat a cough with laxatives!* And the clerk says, *Oh yeah? Look at him. He's afraid to cough!*"

Geoff and I are the only ones who laugh. Markus and Donny probably can't hear over the music. Sean's focused on rolling.

Geoff takes a hit from the flask, passes it back to me. At first this stuff tasted harsh without pop, but it's going down just fine now. I hold it out to Sean.

Heavy metal blares. Markus twists around in his seat. "Coming down. I'll have some of that," he shouts and snatches the flask.

"Hey man, give it here," Donny yells.

Geoff leans across me and smacks the back of his head. "Not when you're driving, dumb-ass."

"Yes, Mother."

Sean lights the joint. Maybe I'll just have one toke.

After the joint makes its way around the car, Donny yells, "Landing at Burger Kink."

Suddenly, I'm hungry.

Burger Kink is all fries, vinegar, windows, and chrome, with a long counter and a few tables. I order before remembering I don't have even a lousy cent on me. So, instead of waiting for my food, I head for the can hoping they'll forget about me. I'm feeling kind of fractured since getting out of the car. The floor slants down to the left, but I'm okay if I lean a bit to the right. I take a piss, then go into a stall, sit with my eyes closed for a while. That scrambles my stomach so I get back up, splash water on my face, and slip out again. The floor seems to be slanting the other way now.

The boys aren't in the restaurant. Five girls gab away at a table across the room. A plump one whose hair reminds me of a pineapple looks over at me. She says something and then all the girls take a peek my way. I wave, cool-like. They burst into laughter.

I call, "Floor's tilted!" figuring that'll explain everything. Then, while I'm checking that my zipper's up, the man behind the counter says, "Hey, Red! Your order's ready."

"Ooops. I'll be back." I nod then slide out to the parking lot. In the fuzzy, white light from Burger Kink's window, I see everybody on the far side of the lot. Donny's talking to four guys who have their backs to me. Markus stands off to the side, stiff, like a little statue bolted to the ground. Geoff and Sean sit on top of a picnic table watching Donny and the others while they shove food into their faces.

Maybe Geoff will give me a few fries. I head toward him, weaving around a parked car then using the white lines on the pavement to help navigate.

As I get closer, Donny shakes his head. He's talking to the littlest guy who has a ponytail straggling down the back of his leather jacket. I can't hear anything over the sound of passing cars until I'm almost in front of Geoff's table. Then one of the other four guys says, "We know you fuckin' cheated us."

Donny smiles. "No, man. You've got me wrong."

The guy with the ponytail says, "No, you got me wrong." His voice is high, like a girl's.

Donny's smile twitches. He scratches his chin. "Carl, I did not rip you off."

Even though the ponytail — Carl — lowers his voice, I hear, "I know you cut my stuff." He's got this soft voice that gives me the creeps. I straighten up, try to focus. Take a step closer.

Donny puts his hands up beside his shoulders, as though surrendering. "No, man. I swear."

Carl says, "So, just to be fair, I'm gonna cut you."

Geoff and Sean freeze, burgers halfway to their mouths.

Carl reaches behind his back. His fingers curl into a fist. Something glints above his belt.

"Shit!" I pitch forward, grab his arm. "Knife!" Adrenalin shoots through my body.

Everyone starts moving. I snap Carl's closed fist back. His grip loosens and the knife falls. I let go of Carl, lunge for the knife, and accidentally kick it. It skitters over the black asphalt.

I'm in the middle of a blur of squirming bodies. Someone grabs my shoulder. I pivot dizzily, swinging with both arms. Everything's spinning. My fist connects with flesh and someone shouts, "Fuck!"

A leather-covered arm slams into my stomach like a battering ram. I reel backward, get shoved hard from behind. Everything in my stomach rushes up my throat, roars out of my mouth. I trip. My knees slam onto pavement. Pain bolts through me. Then, black.

Next thing I know, someone's hauling me up.

"Come on, Seb!" It's Geoff.

A long way off, sirens sound.

Geoff pushes my head down and shoves me into the back seat beside Sean. My stomach feels knotted and my knees are burning. Markus is in the front, laughing like a maniac.

Donny's beside the car. "You saw it," he shouts. "They fuckin' started it!"

"Who's he shouting at?" I ask.

"Gawkers," Geoff says, squashing in beside me.

Sean yells, "Let's go!"

Donny's head cracks against the car roof before he drops into his seat, swearing.

Sean leans over me, yells, "Don! Get it together!"

The engine revs. We jerk forward, bounce over a curb, and peel off down the road. I take some deep breaths, smell sweat and vomit. Still, I feel better since barfing.

Donny rubs his forehead, hoots over Markus' crazy laughing. "We showed those motherfuckers! You're the man, Geoff."

Geoff tries to twist around, but it's too tight. "Are the cops following us, Don?"

Cops? I listen hard for the sirens.

Donny looks in the rear-view mirror. We take a corner without slowing. Markus' head whacks the window. He stops laughing.

Sean digs his elbow into my ribs. "Get off me."

Geoff says, "Slow down, man!"

Markus is laughing again.

I hear sirens, try looking back. "The cops are coming." Everything's spinning. "Oh, shit."

"What do you care?" Sean asks, pressing a serviette to his bloody chin. "Don's the one driving his old man's car without a licence."

I think I'm gonna puke again.

Donny punches Markus' shoulder. "Shut. The fuck. Up!" Markus stops his noise. When Donny puts his hand back on the wheel I notice his rings. They aren't sparkling now.

The sirens fade.

Donny says, "No problem, boys. We're home free. Geoff, you gotta teach me that kung fu shit. And, Sebastian, good move with the blade."

"Yeah," Sean says. "And brilliant timing with the barf."

I'm about to say, *Very funny*, when Geoff says, "Yeah. The one you spewed all over took off like a scared monkey."

"I didn't know it hit anyone," I say.

Sean throws his balled up serviette at my head. "Wipe your face, man. You're gross."

Donny says, "This calls for a celebration."

Really? What if the police got the license plate?

Markus whoops.

Sean says, "Time for a blunt."

I twist around to look out the back again.

Geoff nudges me. "Chill out."

I nod, figure things could be worse, but Donny knows what he's doing.

Thirteen

By the time I wobble home on a bicycle borrowed from Donny, I've been lost twice, skinned my hand falling off the bike, and puked up all my victory drinks. I stumble up the back steps wishing Donny had just given me a drive home. A light comes on as the door opens.

"Sebastian! What's happened? Are you all right? Can you manage?" Ford grabs my arm like I'm some kind of invalid. "What's that smell? Were you sick?"

Too many questions.

She leads me to the kitchen table. "Good Lord. Something tells me you're going to be a wreck tomorrow, too." Her forehead is a mess of wrinkles.

"Don't worry, Ms. Ford." My words seem to be coming out slower than usual. "I'll be behher soon."

She sits me down. "I wondered why you were so late. Stay there. I'll be right back."

I'm not going anywhere. I plant my forehead on the tabletop. Close my eyes. Feel the floor, my chair, the table, everything tip up then down, spin around and around. I'm going to barf again. I lift my head. Everything slides to a stop.

Ford reappears. Sturdy. Grey.

"Grey?" she says.

"Did I say that? Or . . . are you some kind of mind reader?" I smile, but she just shakes her head.

"Let's get those cuts cleaned." She wipes gravel out of my bloody palm then fixes a mess on my chin. Her face seems to sag. I know that look: disappointment. And suddenly I remember her smile from the last time I saw her, eons ago, when she hassled me about when I'd be back.

I gulp, tears stinging my eyes. I can't believe I'm stinkin' drunk. "I'm sorry. I'm soo, sooo sorry." My arms cushion my head's fall.

⌒

Early Saturday morning, I'm bent over the toilet bowl, stomach bucking, head pounding. Nothing's coming up, but I can't stop heaving. Feel like the cracked sole on the used shoes Jim gave me for Christmas. Swear I'll never drink another drop. How could I do that, after Dad-A-Dick?

Finally, I grope my way back to the bedroom. Easing myself into bed with a scraped hand and sore knees, I see a reddish-black bruise glaring above my boxers. I remember the punch, puking, one of the guys calling me gross. I pull the covers over my head.

Despite my misery, sleep keeps slipping away. I remember the pinball at Donny's. The girl with the pineapple hair at Burger Kink. The knife. Geoff laughing. Being crammed in the car. Ford's sad face.

Shit! She had to know I was drunk. How could I have been such an idiot? And how did I make it to bed?

A knock on the door ricochets through my brain like a Jackpot ball. I open my eyes, squint at the clock. 10:00 AM. Guess I slept after all.

"Yeah?" My eyelids feel like pillows.

The door opens. Ford peers in. "Awake?"

I nod, and my brain slams against my skull — massive bumper shot.

Ford's not smiling. "This will help." She hands me a glass of water.

I prop myself up on an elbow to take the water, just 'cause she's not yelling. Once the first sip's down, I gulp the rest. She watches, her lips pressed tight.

I want to say, *Sorry 'bout last night,* but when I open my mouth, nothing comes out but a rotten stink.

Ford takes the glass. "We'll talk when you're feeling more like yourself."

I slump back down. She closes the door.

Wish I'd said thanks.

By eleven o'clock, I'm still weak and hurting, but I make it to the bathroom for a leak without holding onto the walls. Feel slightly more human after brushing the crust off my teeth and tongue.

Last night's clothes are lumped at the foot of my bed. When I bend to pick them up, the sour smell of weed and vomit makes me gag. I don't even remember undressing.

Shit! Ford's gotta know I smoked dope too.

Suddenly I'm sweating. Did she call Hassles? This could be the end. Doomed to a group home. After that, no home. I sit on the edge of the bed, force myself to breathe deep. In for four seconds. Out real slow. After a while my heart stops racing.

Ford's not happy, but she didn't shout. Maybe she didn't call Hassles yet. Maybe she'll let me stay. Besides, it's not like tons of guys don't party. Her own kid probably got drunk or stoned once in a while. And I'm not her first foster kid.

I dress, trying not to move my head, then creep into the kitchen. No sign of her. I check the living room. Not there.

What? She left without telling me? After all the *common courtesy* speeches? I tell myself to chill, slog back to the kitchen for water. At the sink, something orange outside catches my eye: Ford on her knees in the backyard.

She looks up, flaps a giant orange hand.

I take one last deep breath. Time to find out what's next.

Replaying Hassles' group home lecture, I shove through the back door. Sun pierces straight to my brain, incinerating all thought beyond basic survival. I lurch across the yard, one hand raised as a visor, the other holding my glass.

Ford's unwrapping brown cloth from a bush. "Time to take the burlap off these bushes. Feeling better now?"

"Ah-ha." My stomach feels like a scrunched-up plastic bag.

"I hope that was a yes." She settles onto her heels. "Want to sit?"

Hard to imagine pulling that off without spazzing out.

"Here." She pats a puny mat with her oversized glove. "You can sit on this."

Without a hope of touching down on Ford's landing pad, I fold like a rusted chair, then set what's left of the water on the grass and stare at the ground.

"I was worried about you last night, Seb."

I grunt. No one worries about me. I figured that out ages ago.

"We had an agreement. Want to tell me why you were two hours late?"

"Two hours? I didn't mean to be late."

"But you were." Her voice is heavy.

My glass is on a bump, leaning away from me and sparkling painfully in the sun. I go to fix its drunken tilt but my hand's shaking too bad.

"I'm sorry." I stop talking before my voice crumbles.

After a moment, Ford says, "I'm not going to play games with you, Seb. When you were late, I called the Malner's house several times. No one answered."

"I was wrong about Donny's plan. We went out for burgers."

"I wish it had been nothing more than that." She sighs. "I've got a good nose, and a good idea of what you were up to."

Here we go — *I'm sorry but, I don't want you . . .*

"Seb? I expect you want to be treated like an adult."

"I guess." My brain feels like it's being shrink-wrapped.

"You know part of that means assuming responsibility for your actions, right?"

I nod. *I'm* the one with the killer hangover and fist-sized bruise. That's assuming responsibility, isn't it?

"I lost three hours of sleep because of you, Seb." She starts unwinding burlap from another plant. "I think some restitution is in order."

"Restitution?" That's like revenge, isn't it? She's saying straight out that she wants to get even? "So, what are you going to do?" I ask.

Her eyes open wide. "Seb! The question is what are *you* going to do?"

"I'm not going to do anything!" Is this a trick?

"Well, that attitude worries me even more." She frowns. "Do you understand what I'm talking about?"

The throbbing in my head is so loud it's like I'm standing in the middle of a storm. I can't think. I nod, *Yes*, and wait, hoping I'll understand what she says next. But she doesn't say anything for a while.

Finally, she says, "You and I are a team of sorts."

"We are? We just eat, do dishes, and watch TV together."

She sighs. "Exactly. We have to work together so we're both happy."

"Happy?" Except being baked with Donny for an hour or so, I can't recall any *happy*. Lots of *wishful*. And *worried*. Same with *angry* and its random eruptions. *Horny*'s pretty much a constant. The more I try to think of *happy*, the bigger the hollow inside me grows.

"What is this bullshit?" bursts out of me.

Ford sucks in a breath, but she doesn't look as surprised as I am. She's got one of those strange looks I can't figure.

I swipe my hand over my face. "Sorry — again."

She sighs. "Let's get back to restitution: I propose that you take over doing laundry for nine weeks. It shouldn't take more than twenty minutes a load. That adds up to my lost three hours."

So, she's not getting rid of me — yet. The pounding under my skull eases.

"Does that sound reasonable to you, Seb?"

"Yeah!" Hardly revenge. I pick up my glass, start to push myself up.

"Just a minute."

"Huh?" I sink back.

"You've got to remember: your court appearance is just . . . "

"Ten days away." And I do not want to think about it. "So, what? You're worried I'll be jailed before the laundry deal's done?"

Her lips twitch, like maybe she's stifling a smile. Then she frowns. "No! Did you consider what would have happened had the police found you drunk, stoned, or fighting last night?"

My hand jerks and the water left in my glass splatters over my leg. "How do you know . . . "

"I couldn't help seeing that nasty bruise on your stomach."

"Oh."

"Seb, I'm guessing that your friend's behaviour was also inappropriate — reprehensible, in fact."

"Repre-what? He didn't hit me."

She shrugs. "Someone gave you liquor and marijuana, and who knows what else. I'm guessing that someone was this Donny fellow."

I'm about to say she's wrong when she says, "Please. I don't appreciate being lied to."

She could be a mind reader.

But the weirdest thing is, all this time she's stayed calm. Not Psycho-Dad-calm, ready to snap like a mouse trap. Just like matter-of-fact calm. Not that she could whip me like the Psycho even if she wanted to, now.

"Seb, I can't control who you choose as friends. But I must warn you: choose wisely. Your teachers, the police, almost everyone, will judge you not only by your own behaviour, but by your friends."

"But that's not fair." My voice squeaks.

She sighs. "Perhaps not. But that's life." She clears her throat. "You've got some real strengths — such as your ability in math — that could take you to college in a couple of years." She must see my surprise on my face, because she shrugs. "Your teacher called. Apparently Ms. Burk enjoys reporting good news." Her eyebrows go up. "I hope you'll be the one to share in the future."

Really? "Yeah. Sorry." One more for the foster-parent firsts list.

"Anyway, getting back to what I was saying." Mrs. Ford nods. "You're a good kid. And I strongly urge you to stay away from this Donny."

Anger flashes through me. "Well, you're wrong about him. He's a great guy."

"I don't want to see you land in any more trouble."

"I won't."

Ford shakes off the orange gloves. "I'm finished here. Can you help me up?" For the first time since I came home yesterday, she cracks a little smile. "Or should I be helping you?"

I push myself up, saying, "I've got it," with a clenched jaw.

She stretches out a hand covered with bulging blue veins. I've never touched anyone old as her before. I reach with my good hand. Hers feels surprisingly smooth, soft. And strong, as her fingers wrap tight around mine. With one pull, she's up.

I trudge back to the house, squinting against the light. She can't stop me hanging with Donny.

She goes into the garage to stash her gardening junk. My gaze runs over its outside wall. Something's wrong.

Donny's bike! I swear I left it there last night.

"Mrs. Ford, did you put the bike away?"

"What bike?" she calls from inside the garage.

Fast as I can with a shrunken brain and wobbly legs, I scramble around the garage, scan the driveway, the road. It's got to be here somewhere! I even hurry around the old car parked inside the garage before going back out to stare miserably at the wall where I left it.

Donny's bike is gone.

⟳

I can't handle dragging myself over to his place with the bad news till Sunday. So, after putting a load of laundry in the washer and digging out Ford's new flower bed, I wash up and head out.

"Where are you off to, Seb?" Ford asks from the living room.

I almost blurt, *Donny's,* but catch myself. "Thought I'd check out the mall. Back in a couple hours."

Her newspaper rustles. "All right. I'll see you later."

With only a twinge of guilt, I pull the front door shut behind me.

Skinny doesn't show, so I go alone. The whole lousy way I wonder how much the bike was worth, what Donny will say, how I'll pay him back, and if this is the end of being his friend.

When I finally get there, a tall lady opens the door. I remember Donny's mom from little league. "Hi, Mrs. Malner." I say. "I'm Se — "

"Can I help you?" She gives me a snooty stare.

I clear my throat. "Is Donny home?"

"Just a minute. Donny!" She closes the door.

I wait, gazing down at the door knocker. Never really noticed it before. It's a sleek, oval ring with a flat diamond the size of my thumbnail at the bottom. Suits Mrs. Malner.

Donny opens the door. "Sebastian!" He steps onto the porch, half smiling, half frowning. "What's up?"

Sean comes out behind him. "Is he going, too?"

Donny shakes his head.

"Going where?" I ask hopefully.

Donny shrugs. "Nowhere. So?"

I swallow. "So, bad news."

He doesn't say anything.

"About your bike — "

He glances around, probably looking for it. "Just bring it to school."

Sean says, "What bike? You get a new bike?"

New? Figures I have to lose a new bike.

"No. It's not that." I swallow. "It's — "

"It's what? Spit it out, Sebastian!"

"Somebody stole it."

Donny doesn't shift a muscle. Just looks at me, real cool. "No shit?" After a moment, he says, "Well, I didn't use it . . . much." He gives me a kind of sad smile. "Probably can't replace it, though."

Sean goes back inside like he owns the joint.

Donny leans against a pillar, rubs a finger over his chin for a bit. "It cost a fair chunk."

"I'll pay for it, Don." I talk fast. "How much was it worth? I'm broke right now, but I can get a job, pay you . . . "

"Don't sweat it, man." He shrugs. "Let me think on it. I'll get back to you. Listen, I'd invite you in, but I'm pretty busy." He reaches for the door.

"Sure. No problem." I've got this crappy feeling, like I just tilted the game. I plod down the steps and head home.

A fair chunk. Wish I knew exactly what that means.

Wish Skinny had come.

Fourteen

Despite Nina's enthusiasm, by Friday my glacier report seems less than pointless, and I can't stop thinking I'll never see Mr. Frogley again. After wussing out during my visits with him Monday and Wednesday, I resolve that today I tell him about my court date in four days, no matter how disappointed he'll be.

I make a quick pit stop at Ford's to drop my books and snatch a raw hamburger from the fridge. "Going out for a while," I say as I pass her in the living room.

"Again?" She looks up from a cookbook. "That makes — what? — five or six times in the last week and a half. You haven't been getting together with that Donny?"

I wish. "No, I haven't," I say, nerves jangling.

I'm not telling her that my best buddies right now are a dog and an old guy I know from grade three.

"Good." Before she's done sticking her glasses back on, I'm out of there. As the front door swings shut, she calls, "Be home . . . "

"For dinner by seven," I call back.

I haven't gone half a block when Skinny appears, ribs sticking out as much as ever. "Knew I'd see you. Nobody's feeding you but me. Eh, boy?" I give him a good rub. "I'm sure gonna miss you if I catch shit next week."

I pull the meat from my pocket. He cocks his head to one side, like he's asking a question.

"No, I never ask, 'cause she'd say no. Foster parents don't feed anyone's dog but their own. They're all just in it for the money." Although, she did buy me some brand new clothes.

I unwrap the plastic. Skinny's tail whips back and forth. He leaps to catch the meat and I drop the balled-up plastic through a grate. "Come on."

We're a block past my old home when there's a shriek and a skateboard zips across my path.

"You okay?" I call to the kid lying flat on her back at the edge of the old skate park.

"Oops. Ouch." A little girl with a million short braids sits up. "My bad. I kind of lost control."

"I can relate."

She rubs her bottom and gives me a lopsided smile. "I guess I'll be okay. Unless my big brother finds out I used his board."

"Good luck with that." I shove it back to her and then jog the rest of the way to Fairhaven.

Mr. Frogley is near the fence way across the schoolyard, chucking crap into an oversized plastic bag slumped on the ground. Seeing me, he straightens, gives his lower back a rub.

"Hey, Seb. What's cookin'?"

I shrug. "Not much. 'Cept . . . "

"Except what?"

When I don't answer, he says, "I can see you got somethin' heavy on your mind."

"Yeah." I watch Skinny sniffing around.

Stepping into Traffic

Mr. Frogley hands me a garbage bag and some work gloves. "Put those on," he says, then goes back to picking up empties.

Dropping ketchup-smeared cardboard into the bag, I say, "Don't want the dog eating this."

We shuffle along by the fence, tossing garbage into our bags without saying anything for a bit. Then he holds up some girl's underwear as though it were a dead skunk. "I call this corner of the yard Sin Central. Over the years, I've found everything here — food, clothes, condoms, switchblade knives, needles, you name it."

"Cool."

"Hmm. That's not how I'd put it." He rubs his back again. "So, you going to tell me what's troubling you?"

Whichever way things go, this could be the last time I hang with him. I gaze at the brown grass. "I ended up back in this 'hood 'cause I was caught shoplifting."

"Eh? What's that you said?"

I clear my throat. "I got caught shoplifting."

"Oh. Learnin' the hard way, eh? When?"

I catch my breath. *Learning?* "When I lived at my last foster home."

"Well, you're not the first youngster to make a mistake." He shrugs. "I wondered why CSC would move you to a new school in February." He doesn't look or sound surprised. "So — you want to tell me about it?"

I end up telling him everything: all about Chris and me, what happened the day I got busted. Even about Jim, Betty, Maggie, and Little J.

We've picked up every last sign of sin by the time I'm at the end of my story. "If things go bad in court, I'll probably have to leave here, too."

Mr. Frogley ties his garbage bag. "I doubt things will go bad as you imagine."

I hope he's right.

We walk toward the school. "When do you go to court, Seb?"

"Next Tuesday."

His eyebrows go up. "Well, I'm sure pleased you shared your story. Believe me, a couple mistakes don't mean you're a bad guy." He heaves his bag into the dumpster at the edge of the parking lot. "You got some more time?"

I nod. Skinny sidesteps around the bin, his nose shoved under it, exploring.

"Then come on. I've got some sweeping to do inside."

We head for the side door. Skinny trots over as though he wants to come with us. I give him a quick pat. "Stay outside. I'll be back."

Mr. Frogley unlocks the door and I follow him in. "Hold on — I'll grab the supplies."

I've helped Mr. Frogley in here enough now that I'm not near losing it. Everything's the same as when I was in grade three, but different. The hallway is still the colour of day-old mustard, but it feels smaller. The classroom desks have been replaced by chairs with tiny writing tablets. And the blackboards are mostly whiteboards now.

"Okay, here you go." Mr. Frogley's got a broom in one hand, a small bucket of sawdust in the other. He hands me the broom and sprinkles sawdust on the floor.

I smile. "I always wanted to try this."

He snorts. "Believe me, it ain't as excitin' as it looks."

As we sweep down the hall, he says, "Okay. I'm gonna give you some tips to impress the judge."

Impress the judge. "I never even thought of that!" I look over at Mr. Frogley. "How do you know anything about that?"

"Well, Seb, I wasn't always the upstanding citizen you see before you now. Fact is, it took me a while to learn my lesson."

"Oh?" Trying to hide my surprise, I focus on the sawdust shuffling along in front of my broom. "What lesson?"

"You got to think ahead on the upshot of your actions. Because for every action, there's a reaction."

I follow him into the gym where he puts down some more sawdust. "My big brother and some of his old boys — they weren't real bad. Just not the brightest. Hmm?"

I nod.

"But I had enough sense to see the trouble with their crackerjack ideas — like stealing outdoor Christmas lights and selling them to neighbours."

He stops talking, so I glance at him. He's leaning on his broom, staring up at the ceiling. "Or," he says, "like pretending to be furnace inspectors to get into big houses." He shakes his head. "But, my brother never wanted to hear from me. So, I'd end up taggin' along, just hopin' to keep him out of trouble." Mr. Frogley's voice goes soft. "I never did, though and — long story short — I ended up in a heap of my own.

"So, Seb." He frowns and waits till I'm looking him in the eye. "One lesson here is, stay away from anybody." His voice gets louder. "And by that, I mean anybody who's going to be a bad influence. You hear me?"

I sigh. "Yes, sir." Sounds like Ford.

K.J. Rankin

"Good." Still staring he says, "You'll know who they are."

"Yes, sir."

"Okay." He starts sweeping. "So. Impressing the judge." His voice is back to normal. "First impressions — very important. You already got a pretty clean-cut look to you, but no gum chewing or nail biting in court."

"Right."

"Look the judge in the eye. Stand straight. Hands out of your pockets. Speak up. Say, *Sir*. Or, *Ma'am*, if you get a lady. Hmm. Oh yeah! Say you're sorry for what you done."

I stop sweeping, stare at Mr. Frogley. I'm sorry I got caught, but . . .

As though he knows what I'm thinking, he says, "Seb, your parents got taken early, but they were around long enough for you to know they weren't raising you to be a thief! They had *much* higher hopes."

I sigh, look down at my broom, and nod.

"And you tell that judge you're already volunteering to make up for what you done."

"But I'm not!"

He points at my broom. "You've been helping me since the second time you came around. Nobody's paying you. I'll write a letter saying that."

"Thanks, Mr. Frogley." I swallow the lump in my throat. "You're great."

He snorts, shrugs, and then smiles.

We dump the sawdust and hang the brooms up in his office, a giant closet filled with cleaning supplies and an old, scratched-up desk. Mr. Frogley sits at the desk, pulls a sheet of paper from a drawer. The school's name and address are in green at the top — real official. After thinking a bit, he starts writing. I lean against the wall, wondering what he'll say. Maybe I won't end up in juvie thanks to Mr. Frogley.

A couple minutes later, he hands me the letter, folded into an envelope. "There you go, sir."

"Thanks!" It's not sealed.

"Remember, especially if you hear *alternative measures,* give them that letter."

"Alternative measures. Whatever that is."

"It's good. They figure out a better punishment for you than being locked up."

"Sure hope I hear *alternative measures* on Tuesday."

On our way out, Mr. Frogley says, "Hold up a minute!" He hurries back into his office. Half a minute later, he's back. Grinning, he hands me a black clip-on tie. "You can borrow it. I keep it for impressin' the inspector. Make you look snappy."

"Thanks, Mr. Frogley." I fold the tie and slide it into my pocket. "Think I had a smaller version of this when I was five."

He gives me the Kermit smile.

We walk out to his car. Skinny comes running from the far side of the field. Mr. Frogley thumps my back. "Good luck next week, Seb. You be sure and let me know how it goes. No matter what happens. Eh?"

The lump's back in my throat. "I will, if I can."

I read the letter on the way home. It says how Mr. Frogley knew me way back when. That I've helped him clean for at least ten hours since coming back. The letter says, *Seb has proven to be a good, hard worker, even though I've never paid him a cent.*

109

I'm swinging along, feeling taller, stronger than ever. Skinny's trotting just to keep up. "I'm not so worried about my trial, Skinny. I've got this weird feeling — almost like I'm happy?"

Good old Mr. Frogley.

Fifteen

Monday, I spend most of lunch working on the glacier report while rain beats steadily against the library windows. In *Mighty Glaciers,* I come across the word 'till.' 'Till' is *glacial debris — stones, bushes, loose earth — nature's garbage.* The book says, *Till is either pushed forward, brushed aside, or pulled along on the glacier's journey.* I think about all the shitty foster homes, lost friends, new schools. I'm living Till.

Then, on the Internet, I find tons of info about the effects of glaciers melting real fast thanks to global warming. Depressing stuff, from the likely extinction of penguins in the Antarctic to millions of people being forced to move 'cause their homes will be underwater. Sort of puts things in perspective.

I take a break before class to hang with Nina and Matt. The rain means the caf is totally packed, so we end up on the hall floor near my locker. Beside me, Matt flips through *Riff* magazine. Across the hall from us, Nina devours a cream-filled donut while dictating who should say what about glaciers, as if anyone besides Waldozer will be listening.

"Look at this!" Matt holds up his magazine, open at an ad for a drum set. "Sweet, eh?"

I shrug. "Five digits?"

He sighs. "Some day . . . "

Nina swallows her last bit of donut and peers around a couple pairs of passing legs. "You should go to one of Matt's gigs, Seb. His band is excellent."

"Maybe I will." He looks so square, no tattoos or crazy hair. How hot could he be?

"Capt'n Crunch, his band, played at the animal shelter's Christmas party."

"Animal shelter?"

"Where she works," Matt says.

"Part-time." Nina opens a chocolate milk. "And at the Christmas party — "

"Hey, Sebastian!" Donny calls over the heads of a bunch of kids in the hall.

As I scramble to my feet, Nina says, "Don't tell me you're friends with him!"

I say, "Hope so," at the same time Matt says, "Mind your own business, Nina."

Nina shoots Matt an angry look just before Donny steps in front of me, blocking her.

"Hey, Don," Nina says in a fake friendly voice. "How's business?"

Donny ignores her. "I've been looking for you, man."

"Me too. So what — "

"Let's go." He glances in Nina's direction. "Parking lot."

"Okay. I'm right behind you. Just gotta stash this stuff in my locker."

"Cool." He strides towards the back door.

I catch Nina and Matt exchanging frowns.

"You'll get soaked with that big jerk," Nina says.

"He's not a jerk."

"Nina, mind your own . . . "

"Okay, okay!" She crushes her empty milk carton. "And Seb — about our geography presentations — you should do *till*. After all, that's you, right? Sebastian Till."

I wait a moment, but she doesn't wink.

"Right," I say, then stride down the hall after Donny.

Three minutes later, I'm squashed into the driver's seat of some random little car in the school parking lot. Rain streams down the windshield. A curling pine tree air freshener dangles from the rear-view mirror — any smell it had, long gone.

In the passenger seat, elbows pinned to his sides, Donny rolls a joint. "So thoughtful of people to leave their cars unlocked."

"You really don't know whose it is?" I crane my neck, looking through the back window for the owner to appear any moment. "You sure it's cool?" I can't believe the day before court, I'm committing another crime.

Donny finishes rolling. "Relax." He lights the joint, takes a long toke. "It's not like we're stealing it."

"Why don't we talk over in the trees?"

Donny wheezes. "In the rain?"

The car is filling with smoke. "I'm gonna stink." What if Waldozer smells it? Now we're fogging up. "And I can't open the power window. If you really don't know who this car belongs to — "

"Quit . . . " Donny inhales, " . . . being a girl."

Déjà heard. My jaw stiffens.

Donny holds the joint out to me. When I hesitate, he says, "Think about it. You ever see anyone leave here at the *end* of lunch?"

"I guess not." I take a tiny little toke. "I go to court tomorrow. Don't want any more trouble right now." I pass the joint back.

"Oh?" Donny tokes.

I nod. "You ever been?"

"Not me." He rifles through the glovebox. "Wonder who this heap belongs to."

A bunch of wet-wipes, small Band-Aids, and a comb are wedged in with the owner's manual. The car probably belongs to a mom with little kids.

"So, what'd you figure the bike was worth, Don?"

Leaving the glove box open, Donny takes another long drag. "You have fun the other night?"

"When?"

"You know, man!" He's got a big grin. "Burger Kink. The boys."

"Oh! Yeah. Sure. Adrenalin rush." I laugh. "It was great. The bruise on my stomach is already turning yellow."

"Wild, eh?" Donny takes another puff. "See Geoff do his kung fu thing?"

"Not really."

"Yeah — I guess not. At least you made it home before losing the bike."

"It was stolen, not lost." The yawning glovebox bugs me.

Donny passes the joint my way again. "Anyhow, I was thinking you could do something for me, Sebastian. In exchange for the bike."

"What?" I pass the joint back without toking.

"No biggie. Just pick something up for me on Saturday."

"What?" I hold my breath — ready to say *no* to drugs.

He scratches his chin. "Just a bit of money."

I let my breath out. "Who from?"

"Some guy who owes me four hundred."

"Four hundred dollars?" Duh. No, jellybeans, idiot. "That's *a bit*?" I take a deep breath. "Listen, Don, I don't want to be part of Sean and your *biz*."

Donny stares at me a moment. "Nina been talking about me? She had a crush on me." He holds the joint out again. "Anyhow, Sebastian. I told you, it's no biggie. And I don't want you to be part of the biz either."

I ignore the joint. "Oh? Then, why don't you do it yourself?"

"The timing's bad for me, man." He rubs the stubble on his chin. "My parents are forcing me to go to some fucking family bullshit thing."

"So, get it a different day." The smoke is stifling.

Donny takes another toke. "The derelict gets paid late Friday, and he can't hold onto his money. If I don't collect right away, I'll never get paid. It's just for a few weeks."

"A few weeks? He's paying a bit each week?"

Donny exhales slowly. "I mean, it's just a few Saturdays — maybe three, five."

"Come on, Don." And, what *family thing* goes on for weeks?

"The guy lives on Braemar, not far from here," Donny says. "You get the money, then wait until I'm home." He flicks the ashes. "Then, you come over, give me the cash, and we party at my place." He grins. "I'll see if any babes are interested. And don't worry, Sebastian. Really,

115

buddy." He brushes a finger over his chin. "I wouldn't ask you to do this little favour if I thought you'd have any trouble with it."

"I don't know, Don."

"Sebastian, you're a guy I can trust." He shrugs. "I just thought, you seem to like partying, and since you lost the bike . . . I've got your back, man; but, if it's a big problem — " He shakes his head.

"Okay. I guess I can do that." I try to breathe steady. "And then we're even, right?"

"Right." He smiles. "Want the last toke? Forget it." He drops the roach between his feet. "Filter."

After telling me exactly where and when to pick up his money, he says, "So, you sure you're down with that?"

I nod.

"Cool. Later, man." He climbs out, slams the door, and heads for the school.

I'm halfway out of the car, sucking in fresh air and wondering what exactly I've gotten myself into, when I remember the glovebox. Looking back, I catch my reflection in the rear-view mirror. My eyes look a little puffy. I reach to close the glovebox, and then see the roach. Another creepy message for the car's owner. Bending to grab it, I bonk my shoulder on the steering wheel. The horn blares.

Heart pounding, I spring away from the car, flick the roach into a puddle, and — bent double — scuttle away between the parked cars. Rain pelts down on my back.

I'm already late for Geography.

Don's a good guy. He's got my back.

⤳

At 3:45 PM, I'm dumping the afternoon's textbooks into my locker when Nina hurries up to hers.

She pulls out her knapsack. "I bet you're relieved you didn't end up in the office."

"Huh?"

"You showed up late and stoned for Geography." She wrenches her violin case from her locker.

"I wasn't stoned."

She snorts. "I covered for you when Walters took attendance. And I told him we're doing a joint presentation."

"Oh? Thanks, I guess." Just to bug her, I say, "So, that's a joint presentation on glaciers?"

"Of course! And I won't be happy if I don't get an A." She smiles. "At least."

"You're kidding, right?" I'm waiting for the wink.

She shakes her head. "And, by the way, Don is not, repeat n-o-t," she says, spelling the word, "a guy you want to hang out with. Why would you?"

"Why would you?"

She frowns. "I wouldn't."

I scan the hall, hoping to see *Mind your own business Matt*. "We played baseball together when we were kids."

"That doesn't mean you have to smoke up with him."

"I know. He just wanted to talk to me 'cause I borrowed his bike and someone stole it."

"*Tale as old as time*," she sings.

"What?"

"He probably stole the bike in the first place then, stole it again from you. By the way, you need that book for Math, and I'm hoping you'll help me tomorrow during in-class homework."

"Maybe." I pull the text back out of my locker. "And you're wrong about Don. Why would he steal the bike? The guy lives in a mansion."

Nina snorts. "As if rich kids never lift anything."

"I guess. See you tomorrow."

"Hey — wait a sec!" She closes her locker. Looks like she packed every textbook she owns. "I'm sorry for my *till* remark, earlier. It was totally uncalled for."

I shrug.

"We take the same route, you know. At least, for a while."

"Oh? You've been spying on me?"

She pats her hair and makes a fish face. "Just call me Mata Hari."

I smile. "Who's that? A talking fish?"

Her eyes narrow. "Gee, thanks. Mata Hari was a famous, super-hot World War I spy. That was my sexy imitation."

"Oops."

"Standards were different then. All I really have in common with her is kinky black hair and breasts flat as fried eggs."

Not that flat. There goes my ear. "Oh."

"Of course I wasn't spying." She hefts her bag onto her back. "You just happened to pass me a few times, going so fast, you didn't even notice me." She picks up the violin case then squints. "What's wrong with your ear?"

"Nothing."

"Seriously. Your left ear is really red. Does it hurt?"

"No!"

"You may have an outer ear infection."

"Let's go!"

"Okay. I go right, right about where you meet your dog."

"You mean Skinny." I walk on her left to stop the ear examination. "Not really my dog."

We head outside. The ground's still wet, but the sun is shining. As we walk through the parking lot, Nina asks about Skinny. Then she says, "What are you doing about the bike? Did Don have a fit?"

"No! He was totally cool. When I told him, he said, 'Don't sweat it.'"

"Well," Nina says, "that proves my point: he probably stole it at least once."

"I'm sure he didn't." Maybe he did. It was small for me — would have been small for him. Maybe it was his old bike. Except Sean said it was new.

Nina says, "Still, if I were you, I'd replace that bike. You don't want to feel like you owe him or anything."

I catch my breath, glance at her. It's like she knows what we talked about in the car. I look towards the pine trees. No sign of Donny.

"You going to, Seb?"

"What?"

"Geez! Replace the bike."

"I guess. I'd have to make some money." Why am I hanging with this girl? Why is she hanging with me? I really don't need any more negative shit about Donny.

As Nina blabs about the animal shelter and the cost of spaying pets, my thoughts go in circles. What if I get caught collecting money for Don? What's really wrong with carrying some money around? Why would Don hang with me if I can't even do him a favour? Maybe he's doing *me* a favour, making me feel like I'm paying him back with an easy little job. What could go wrong? How much partying can we do on Saturday afternoons?

Like most days, four blocks from Ford's, Skinny's waiting, tail wagging and tongue flapping.

"Skinny? Yes, you are!" Nina puts down her violin case and scratches behind his ears. "Dogs love my squeaky soprano." She gets his tail going double-time.

She's actually kind of pretty. She's no Tiff. Still . . .

"I love dogs." She straightens up. "Except that they always stick their noses in my crotch. It's so embarrassing."

The crotch comment probably embarrasses me more than any dog ever embarrassed Nina.

"So anyway, Seb, if you're interested, I could ask them at the shelter."

"Ask them?" Did I hear something about finding Skinny a home? Or me a job?

She sighs. "You weren't listening to me, were you?"

"I was." Sort of.

"I guess — like Matt says — I should mind my own business." She shrugs. "This is where we go our different directions. Bye, Skinny." Smiling, she picks up her violin. "See you tomorrow, Seb!" She strides away. Even with that heavy load, she walks with a spring in her step.

I guess I will help her with the math.

That is, if I'm back at school tomorrow.

She stops and calls back, "Your ear's still red. I'd get it checked if I were you."

Sixteen

Next morning, I slog off the bus a block from the courthouse. A few doors along the street, a small bunch of ragged men and women form a sloppy line in front of a closed liquor store. "And it's like fucking five after ten," an old guy missing his front teeth says to the others. On the sidewalk, clumped around each of their feet, dirty bags and boxes overflow with empties.

I speed up.

The dingy, two-storey courthouse has only a couple of pea-sized windows and a front door. Nobody's getting out of there unless they let you. Cops clustered in front remind me of the cockroaches trapped on sticky paper in foster home four.

Only good thing about today — if I'm not locked up once it's over — is I can hang with Chris again. At least on weekends.

I make my way past the cops and smokers, take a poorly-timed breath, and then heave the oversize door open. Now to find Hassles.

A lobby of shining stone walls that look impossibly taller than the building itself takes me by surprise. So does a bullet-headed cop who shouts, "Stop! Backpack on the conveyor belt," before I even notice him or the conveyor belt.

I whip off my pack and dump it on what looks like a grocery checkout counter. It slides through the x-ray machine fastened near the end of the belt. Another cop — small, with greasy, black hair — stands next to a metal door frame set up beside the counter. He waves a cell phone-sized gadget. "Step forward."

I duck through the door frame. It beeps! My stomach churns as though the cops are about to discover a knife or a gun on me. As if.

The short cop moves in close. "Lift your arms."

"I bet you've smelt a lot of sweaty pits." Shut up!

He gives me a bored look. His little metal detector beeps. "What's in your shirt pocket?"

My hand shakes as I show him four quarters.

He waves me on. I grab my knapsack and head down a hall that, minus student lockers, could be any corridor at school. It doesn't seem to belong in the same building as the lobby.

The farther I go, the more crowded the hall gets.

No sign of Hassles.

Except for a few men in suits, almost everyone looks ratty — more like they're waiting for a bus than their day in court. Guess no one gave them Mr. Frogley's "first impressions" speech. They lean against the wall wrung out, depressed, or droop in the few chairs anchored to the floor like park benches.

A man and woman all dressed up rush by, looking important, shoes hammering over the dull hum of voices in the hall. My heart hammers, too, until I glance down at the white shirt Ford found for me, and the shoes from Jim that I shined last night.

Where's Hassles?

Four sets of massive wooden doors spaced along one side of the corridor remind me of the lobby. A sign above the first one says Courtroom One. Which one's mine? Hassles will know.

A couple of women in suits stride past. One of them looks at me. Her snooty glance says I'm no one.

I've gotta hit the can.

I splash water on my face, then remember Mr. Frogley's tie in my pack. I fumble my shirt's collar button through its puny buttonhole, then clip on the tie and hustle back into the hall.

In an alcove filled with mostly occupied chairs across the hall from Courtroom Three, I scan everyone's face. No one's smiling, and no one's Hassles.

Where the hell is she?

And where's the lawyer? Chen. Probably in one of those courtrooms.

I pace back and forth opposite a big, ticking wall clock, pat my back pocket making sure that Mr. Frogley's letter is still there.

The minute hand on the clock jerks forward. Shit! Just five minutes till court!

I whip out of the waiting area, stare down the hall. Two payphones have ridiculously long line-ups. Stinkin' emergency quarters. I should have a cell.

What happens if I miss court? Isn't that called contempt? I could go to jail for that.

Maybe Hassles slipped past me. I rush back, scan the faces again.

Check the clock again. Shit! Two minutes.

"Excuse me!"

It's Ford. She dekes around a large woman with two little kids in tow, and rushes toward me.

"What are you doing here?" I could almost kiss her wrinkled old face.

"It's lucky you're easy to spot! That's a nice tie — just a tad short. Someone from CSC called after you'd gone. Apparently Ms. Haslett had a personal emergency." She's talking so fast, it's hard to keep up. "No one else from the agency could make it today. They said you'd be fine — your case would be deferred."

"Deferred?"

"Postponed."

I groan. "I have to come back again?"

"No. I made some calls. It's irregular, but they're going to let me stand in as your official caregiver and proceed with the case."

"Amazing! Thank you so much, Mrs. Ford."

"Courtroom Four." She's already trucking out of the waiting room. "Hurry, Seb!"

At the last pair of wooden doors, I yank one open and let Mrs. Ford lead the way.

The courtroom has a lot more desks up front than Judge Judy's, and they're on three different levels. The highest desk, right in the middle, is the only empty one. The audience benches are full of little criminals and their tired-looking parents. Mrs. Ford and I find a place in the back row.

She looks around. "You've got some overworked, government-appointed attorney somewhere, Seb."

"That's what Ms. Haslett said when we met her." I check out the people standing at the front. "There! See? Ms. Chen. Black suit, black hair."

Mrs. Ford nods.

A policeman stands beside the highest desk. "Oy-yay, Oy-yay. All rise!"

Once we're up, he makes the kids wearing caps take them off.

I spot Chris' mom near the front beside the aisle. A skinhead stands next to her. It takes me a moment to realize it's Chris. His T-shirt looks new. As though he can feel me looking, Chris turns around and grins.

Makes me smile, too.

His mom elbows him and he faces front again.

The judge — more serious and even older looking than Judge Judy, but wearing the same long, black robe — stumps in and slumps down at the highest desk. The rest of us are ordered to sit. I make sure my tie's straight.

A side door near the front opens. Two police officers steer a stocky guy in handcuffs into the courtroom. He looks too old to be here. He's led to a private seat behind waist-high walls. The handcuffs come off. When he turns around to sit, a few people gasp. Black stitches stretch like a squashed centipede over a red gash down one side of his face.

Turns out, he's up first. I'm not getting everything the lawyers say, but he's one nasty dude. I'm betting he'll be locked up forever. When he gets six months in a group home, I nearly slide off my seat. Wouldn't want to land in *his* home. The cuffs go back on and he's led out of the courtroom.

I wipe my sweaty palms on my pants.

Chris, me, and Alex are called to the front with our adults.

I can't swallow right. Collar's too damn tight.

Chris' grin is gone. He looks scared now. The lady with him and his mom must be a lawyer. I glance back, see Alex saunter up the aisle between two men dressed like the millionaires on *Business Builders*. One looks bored, the other pissed off. The angry one shoves Alex, gets him moving faster. Must be his dad.

Nina's line, *As if rich kids never lift stuff,* comes back to me.

Ms. Chen steps to my side. "Hello, Sebastian. Who's this?" After Mrs. Ford introduces herself, Ms. Chen says, "Good. Maybe we can get this over with today." Smiling tightly, she pulls a sheet of paper from a folder wedged under her arm and scribbles on it.

Another woman, in a creepy black robe like the judge's, says my name. Wish I could just close my eyes and disappear. Instead, I stand up straight as I can and step forward. The woman reads the charges: *Theft under $200. Possession of burglary tools with intent. Break and enter.*

Ms. Chen tells the judge Mrs. Ford is my guardian. The judge frowns, checks out Mrs. Ford and then nods. Ms. Chen hands the page she wrote on to a stony-faced man sitting at a low desk in front of the judge, and then hurries over to a man flipping through a file on the far side of the judge.

I wish I could hear what they're saying.

Mrs. Ford whispers, "The prosecution lawyer — also overworked," just before he looks up from his file.

"The Crown would be willing to accept alternative measures in this instance, your Honour," he says.

Alternative measures. Should I pull out my letter now? Do I at least say I've got a letter? Do I get to talk?

I don't know who to ask. I'm going to miss my chance.

"Sebastian?" The judge glares at me. "Do I have your attention?"

"Yes, ma'am." My knees are trembling so bad, they might buckle.

"Is this the first time you've been in trouble with the law?"

"Yes, ma'am."

"You've never been charged with an offence?"

"No, ma'am."

"I see you've had some bad luck. But, you're lucky to have . . . " She glances at her desk. "Mrs. Ford vouching for you now. Frankly, given the offence and your advanced age, I wouldn't normally consider alternative measures."

"Yes, ma'am. I'm sorry, ma'am." My heart's going like a piston in overdrive. "I've already started volunteering to make up for my crime." I wrench the letter from my pocket. It trembles in my hand. "I have this — Mr. Frogley's letter — about that, ma'am."

Ms. Chen springs around Mrs. Ford as though she was kicked in the butt. She snatches the quivering page, snaps it open, glances at it and passes it along. It goes from one person to another, gets stamped, and passed on again until the judge finally reads it.

Will she want proof I didn't write it myself?

I try licking my lips, but my mouth has gone dry.

The judge puts the letter down. "That's good, Sebastian. However, you'll have to do another thirty hours of community service."

"Yes, ma'am."

She leans forward. "I don't want to see you in this court again." Her eyes drill through me. "Is that clear, young man?"

"Yes, ma'am." Donny's job flits through my thoughts. I try to freeze the look on my face so she won't sense my sudden, sickening doubt.

Ms. Chen writes something in her folder then tucks it back under her arm.

That's it? It's over?

Mrs. Ford whispers, "We wait here for your friends to be dealt with."

It's over! I'm not going to juvie . . . or even reporting for parole! I can keep helping Mr. Frogley.

I feel like gravity's grip just loosened a tiny bit.

It sounds like things are working out the same for Chris, except he has to go somewhere to get a fifty-hour community service assignment because he hasn't done any volunteering yet.

Turns out Alex is not a *mastermind of making easy money*. The bored man has lawyered for him lots, and Alex is not getting alternative measures. He has to come back in three weeks, when the judge will have figured out a suitable punishment.

Ms. Chen hands Mrs. Ford a long yellow sheet of paper. "This has all the information you'll need." She looks at me and smiles — a first. "You surprised me, Sebastian. Good luck."

"Thanks."

She takes another folder from the table behind her.

"*She* just surprised *me*," I whisper to Mrs. Ford.

She smiles. "Let's go, Seb."

Another name is already being called as I follow her down the aisle. I grab my knapsack off the bench and slide out of the courtroom.

In the hall, Alex, his dad, and his lawyer don't even look at me as they push past on their way to the exit. Good riddance.

"Seb! The Ice Man!"

"Chris!" I twist around. The big door swings slowly shut behind him. "How's it going?"

"Going good!" He smiles, points at me. "Wicked gear. Very impressive."

I check my tie. "Thanks. We should hook up some time."

"Yeah! We could . . . "

"You could nothin'." Chris' mom wedges herself through the door. She grabs Chris' elbow, almost yanking him off his feet. "Come on."

As Chris trips along beside her, she says, "I'll wring your ruddy neck if you see either of them boys again. You hear me?"

She meant for me to hear. Chris doesn't look back.

Suddenly, I'm too tired to stand up straight anymore.

Mrs. Ford says, "Come on, Seb."

"That's not fair . . . what she said. It wasn't even my idea."

She shrugs and steers me toward the exit. "You knew it was wrong. And you already know that life isn't always fair. Anyhow, Seb, you behaved well in there. I think the judge was impressed."

It rained while we were in court. I follow Mrs. Ford to her big, old car. Its worn seats smell faintly mouldy. There'd be room for my legs, except that the front seat is practically on top of the dashboard. Mrs. Ford watches the road through the steering wheel; doesn't seem to slow her down any, though.

Trying not to think about Don's bicycle payback or Mrs. Hendrick's "ruddy neck" wringing, I pocket Mr. Frogley's tie, open my collar, and then roll down the window.

Cool air bursts in, whips the stale air out.

Elbow resting on the door, I watch the wet, grey world slide by. Mrs. Ford says, "It's twenty minutes before we reach your school, Seb. Plenty of time to tell me about this Mr. Frogley. I had no idea you were working."

"Neither did I, really." I clear my throat. "Mrs. Ford? I'm glad you showed up today."

She glances at me, smiles. "Me too, Seb. So, tell me about that letter."

Seventeen

A few days later, Mrs. Ford looks at me over the top of her teacup. "Seb, am I feeding you enough?"

I've just stuffed myself with stew, mashed potatoes, and a piece of pecan pie. "Yeah! I've never eaten so much." I dig into my second helping of dessert. "I'm hoping it'll muscle me up. I don't know how you do it — " I stop before saying *with a hundred-year-old munchkin-sized fridge and stove.*

"Hmm." She makes a weird face, like she's puzzled, or angry.

I clue in. Here we go — she's pissed off about me stealing her ham and roast beef for my sandwiches. Not sure why she didn't notice before now, but I knew it was too good to be true. "Your food is awesome!" I talk fast, trying to stall her. "I used to think the food at the Kirbles was great just 'cause Betty mixed it up, but your food is over the top."

She puts her cup down. *"Mixed it up?"*

"You know, the four meal rotation: one night, meatloaf; the next, pancakes; then, hotdogs; then, KD. Like that."

"Oh." She blinks. "I guess I've heard of that. But — "

"'Cause the place before that, I got the same dinner — wieners and beans — every single day of the

131

year." When Chris heard that, he cracked up over the 'fart factor.'

"You're kidding me." Mrs. Ford's smile looks pinched.

I scramble for more to say. "At least it was filling. But what bugged me more, was the place where they never let me and this other foster kid, littler than me, eat with them."

Mrs. Ford closes her eyes for a moment. "I can't imagine what those people were thinking."

"Their real kids always ignored us. Plus, 'Aunty' mostly dished out rice in the back room." Her whispered, *This'll plug you,* always sounded threatening. "She didn't like changing the little guy's diapers." I shrug, and hope Mrs. Ford's forgotten where the food talk was going.

"Good Lord." Mrs. Ford shakes her head. "Anyway, I asked if you're getting enough food because I'm curious. Do you enjoy raw meat?"

"Huh? No!"

"Because some ground chuck, hot dogs, things like that, have been going missing."

"Oh! I thought . . . " It's not about the lunches.

"Hmm?" She stands up. "I'd love to know where it's going, Seb."

"There's a dog," I mumble.

She leans forward. "What did you say?"

"Sorry, Mrs. Ford. But there's this skinny mutt. He doesn't have a collar, and I don't think anyone's taking care of him." I brace for the liar-thief-ingrate lecture.

"You feed a dog." She smiles. "Of course! I should have thought of that."

I nearly tip out of my chair.

"My son did exactly the same thing when he was thirteen."

"The one who went to Alberta?"

"Yes. My only one. Anyhow, we ended up taking in Trixie, a sweet little stray." She gazes at the ceiling for a while. "Jason and Trixie were crazy about each other."

"So, did he take her out west?" I swallow a mouthful of pie.

"No." Mrs. Ford's voice is normal, but her eyes have gone watery. "She would have been alone too much of the time, so he left her with me." She stops a break-away tear.

I pretend not to notice, quit asking questions, and finish my pie. Her dog must've been hit by a car or something.

Mrs. Ford pushes herself up from the table and then clears our plates. "Trixie lived happily for the next twelve years, if you can believe it."

"I guess that's pretty long for a dog?" So why the tears?
"Yes, it is."

For once, her smile doesn't make it up to the wrinkles around her eyes. Either she misses Trixie, or her son out in Alberta. Or maybe both.

As she piles dishes in the sink, I grab a towel, ready to dry.

"So, Sebastian," she says, setting stuff in the drainer. "How about we buy some dog treats for your stray?" Her smile is back to normal — wrinkles all over her face. "They're probably better than what you've been giving him."

"Sure!" I feel as though I just won some sort of prize. Still, I count the black-and-white floor tiles, waiting for her to say that it will cost me.

"Well, perhaps not better, but certainly cheaper." She rinses a plate. "We can do that tomorrow, if you have time after school."

I stop counting and grab a glass to dry. "Sure! Thanks, Mrs. Ford. After the laundry, I can do some other jobs — "

Soon as the word passes my lips, Donny pops into my head and the glass almost slips from my grip.

Skinny doesn't show the next day, but Mrs. Ford and I still go shopping. In *Paws for Pets*, I can't decide what he'd like best. Mrs. Ford asks how big he is, and then starts reading the ingredients listed on different bags. Within five minutes she says, "This one will do, Seb."

I heft the bag of *PROTEIN PACKS Mid-sized Doggy Snacks* up to the cash.

"Excellent choice!" The clerk says, scanning the big bag. "They're pretty pricey, but they really are nutritious." He smiles and takes Mrs. Ford's money.

"Thanks so much, Mrs. Ford. Skinny will love this."

"I hope so."

Back at the car, I put the bag in the back seat and then slide in beside it. "I fit better here."

"Jason used to do the same thing." Mrs. Ford says. "Now do up your seat belt. Are you still willing to do another chore for me?" She looks over her shoulder, eyebrows raised.

"Absolutely!" I've got this good feeling, like everything inside my chest is pushing my ribs out for a change.

"Wonderful." She smiles. "We've got plenty of time to pick up a few plants and get some work done in that new bed before the sun goes down."

Less than an hour later, I'm putting down topsoil. The strong, bittersweet smell of the earth and the stuff waiting to be planted reminds me of Mom.

"What do you think about those two little bushes going there?" Mrs. Ford points.

"Sounds good." While I do that, she carts out a bunch of pots.

"Now we can put in the bulbs that I've been forcing in the basement."

I scatter the last bit of black earth. "Forcing them to what? Go into the pots? Stay in the basement?"

She chuckles. "Forcing them to bloom early, Seb. There's a good chance we'll have daffodils, crocus, and hyacinth flowering here within the next month." She freezes. "Look!" Smiling as though she's found a pot of gold, she points at a blue jay.

Out of nowhere, I hear Mom's voice, *Sebastian, quick! Come here! See the cardinal?*

I lean on my shovel. "My mom got excited about things like that, too."

"She appreciated life's special, little gifts — a sign of a thoughtful soul."

"And she used to love gardening." I use the spade to make tiny holes in the earth. "We had a huge yard with big flower beds stuffed with everything."

"That sounds lovely!" Mrs. Ford works fast, patting bulbs into the fresh holes. "Did you help her in the garden?"

"I'm not sure. But I remember hiding in the flowers when I was playing with my friends."

"My son never liked gardening." She pulls off a glove.

"Oh?"

"This was his ring," she says, pointing at the band on her thumb. "I gave it to him as a graduation gift."

"I thought maybe you wore it for arthritis." Her smile's so sad. I stop breathing. She's going to say he's dead.

"Yes. You mentioned that. No arthritis — yet." She rubs a finger over the gold ring and then puts her glove back on. "He died during his second week on the job in Alberta. It was a fluke accident. That was twenty years ago today."

"Oh." I don't know anything good, or right, to say. "Do you ever think he's watching?"

"No, I don't." Her smile brightens. "But I do believe he's a part of everything around me now — a part of the entire universe."

"I like that idea."

She nods. "He never liked gardening, but he loved flowers, even though he wouldn't admit it to anyone but me or Trixie by the time he went to high school. So, I'm happy that you're here to help me plant some flowers today, Seb."

"Me too." Maybe Mom and Jason are watching us, together.

We get back to planting the bulbs.

When that's done, Mrs. Ford says, "Just one last job now: we're going to put the pansies around the edge of the bed."

And pansies around the edge. Aren't they beautiful, Sebastian?

"Hey!"

Mrs. Ford nearly drops the flat of purple pansies she's handing to me. "What is it, Seb?"

"I *do* remember helping Mom. She said she loved the pansies' little faces. And that even though they look fragile, they're really strong. Right?"

"That's right." Mrs. Ford picks up the yellow ones.

"And I remember she let me mix all the different colours together."

"We've only got the two colours, but go crazy! Arrange them however you want."

I smile. "Even if that's however I can do it fastest?"

She laughs. "However you want."

By the time I head to bed after a snack of leftover pie and milk, I've still got that weird but good feeling from earlier in the day. And I like Mrs. Ford's idea, that Mom and Dad are a part of the universe, around me all the time.

Eighteen

Thursday after school, I go visit Mr. Frogley, tell him how it went down at court.

"Another thirty hours, eh?" He takes the court confirmation form. "Looks like we'll be seeing a lot of each other."

"Yes, sir." I give him the tie. "Thanks for that. I think it helped. And the letter really impressed my lawyer and the judge."

"I'm glad it went well." He gives me a friendly thump on the back. "So, you're going to think twice before you follow anybody into traffic now — right, Seb?"

Don's *small favour* makes me pause. "Yes, sir!" I've gotta quit being paranoid.

"'Cause there'll always be somebody talkin' up some crackerjack idea."

Half an hour later, I'm swabbing a washroom floor when I figure out how to make the first money pickup without Mrs. Ford asking questions. I don't like lying to her. Soon as I'm finished in the john, I go look for Mr. Frogley. He's sweeping out a classroom.

I clear my throat.

He looks up. "Finished already? In that case, grab a broom. You can start on the halls."

Stepping into Traffic

"Sure. But, I was wondering." I lick my lips. "Do you think I could put in some extra hours on Saturdays?"

He stops sweeping. "Well, now. I don't . . . "

"I know you don't work weekends, but I could do all the outside stuff." I talk fast. "I'd do a great job even if you're not here."

He scratches his head. "Don't forget, Seb — I'm union. They've got strict rules which — technically speaking — I'm breaking. I don't know — "

"Working a few Saturdays, it won't take me forever to finish my alternative measures." Soon as I say that, his smile fades, and regret slithers through me. I scramble for the right words. "I mean, I really want to keep working with you, Mr. Frogley. Even after the thirty hours. I just want to have the court stuff finished fast as I can."

After a moment he says, "I guess a few Saturdays would be okay, Seb. Just let me know if anybody comes around asking questions."

"I'll do that. Thanks, Mr. Frogley."

He smiles. "I know I can trust you, Seb."

Guilt nearly gets the truth out of me.

Eleven AM Saturday morning, after telling Mrs. Ford I'll be working at Fairhaven, I start out for Braemar Avenue. I've only gone a block when Skinny shows up and gets the first three of my pocket stock of treats.

We pass people washing their cars, raking leaves from last fall, and planting their gardens. A couple of cyclists go by.

Despite the perfect weather, it feels like a crow's circling in my stomach.

"What's going to happen, eh, Skinny?"

He looks back at me.

"I screw up, Donny'll be pissed off."

Skinny wags his tail. He's not worried. I toss him a couple more treats.

"He never said why the guy owes so much. Must be one serious user."

At the top of Madill, Skinny goes right, as usual. I turn left and seconds later Skinny bounds back my way. After another turn and one more block, I'm at 23 Braemar.

The house, a neat and tidy bungalow smaller than Mrs. Ford's, looks exactly like its neighbours, except that the living room curtains are closed.

"Psycho-Dad used to close the front curtains before he gave one of us shit."

Skinny shoves his snout into my thigh.

"I know. Scary." Plus, I forgot to get the guy's name. "I don't know who to ask for, Skinny."

I climb the front steps.

Just as I'm about to press the bell, the door opens. My heart kicks into overdrive and I jerk backwards.

"You Sebastian?" asks a familiar-looking guy—mid-twenties, with a dark, stubbly beard.

I nod. "Sorry. You kind of surprised me. Donny, Don I mean — "

"Shut up and get in here."

As he moves aside to let me step into a tiny foyer, I remember. He's the driver of the pimped-out car from the day Donny invited me into the woods for a doobie. Don calls this guy a *derelict*?

The guy pushes the door shut, turns to me with the ultimate poker face.

My scalp prickles. "Don sent me to pick up his money."

The guy frowns. "Money? Oh, yeah." His hand slides behind his back. Like Carl, going for his blade at Burger Kink.

I tense.

The guy's hand comes back into view, holding an envelope made of duct tape. "Here it is. Four hundred."

"Oh! I thought . . . " I take the weird envelope. "*Four* hundred?" It's a bit bulky, like four hundred dollars should be, I guess. "But, I thought it was supposed to be a hundred, for four — "

"Whatever. Don't even think about opening it." His eyes look lifeless but dangerous at the same time.

"I wouldn't!" I glance at the door, wishing I hadn't said anything.

He reaches past me, pulls it open, and I know we're done. I cross the threshold and the door clicks shut.

I practically sprint to the sidewalk. Skinny's still standing where I left him. I give him a quick pat. "Just one day, and my payback's finished!" This is good. "Donny'll be happy."

I head for Fairhaven at a jog, fuelled by four hundred bucks in my back pocket. Before starting work, I pat the pocket and almost dissolve when I discover the money has inched its way up, so that it's near falling out. I cram the envelope into my jacket pocket wishing it had a zipper.

After inspecting the dumpster, Skinny lopes across the field to sniff around sin central.

As I work, I check every so often that the money is still in my pocket.

Don trusts me. I'm not blowing this.

∼

Three. Time to unload the cash.

"See you later, boy." I give Skinny a pat, pull the fat envelope from my pocket, take Don's porch steps in one leap, and then bang the gold knocker. Two seconds later, the door flies open.

"Sebastian, my man." Don smiles. "Very punctual. Come on in."

I hold out the envelope. "Here, I . . . "

He frowns, shoves my hand away. "So, you want to play pinball?"

Hoping I haven't screwed up, I shove the money back in my pocket. "I guess so."

Mrs. Malner trudges into the hall carrying a mug and wearing slippers and a big bathrobe, as though she just got up. "Who's this, Donald?"

"Sebastian Till. You remember him. We used to be on the same Little League team."

"Oh?" Mrs. Malner grimaces. Or maybe that's a smile.

"Hi," I say.

"Please excuse me. I have a splitting headache." She heads for the stairs. "Keep the noise down, Donald."

I follow Don down to the basement where he says, "Sorry about this, man. The old bitch was supposed to be out."

Old bitch? Harsh.

He points. "So, let's see what you've got."

I pull the envelope out again and he snatches it. "Did you open it?"

"Of course not," I say, feeling burned. "So, who's coming over?"

Don rubs his chin. "Well, some chicks were supposed to show, but they cancelled."

Shit. "Geoff and Sean?"

He shakes his head.

"What about *party at my place*?" Quick as the words fall out, I want to snatch them back.

Don frowns. "Listen, Sebastian! *You* were doing *me* a favour because of the bike." He knuckle-punches my shoulder. "And you did." His smile is back. "So relax, man."

"You're right. Sorry."

Don points at the dark leather chairs in front of the supersized screen.

I drop into the most amazingly comfortable chair ever.

"You want a drink?"

I shrug. The comforting smell of the leather takes me way back. I close my eyes, see Dad reading his newspaper in a big brown chair while I push my tiny dump truck over and around his blue-slippered feet. I breathe deep, filling the hollow ache for a few seconds.

"Here."

My eyes snap open. "This is like a mini-theatre."

"Sorry. No scotch left."

"No problem."

Don hands me a Coke, then plunks down on the chair beside me. He drops the now-open envelope onto a table.

I sip some pop, point at the envelope. "The guy on Braemar said the whole four hundred's there. So, I figure I'm done with — "

"He's a zombie. You're going back."

"You never told me his name. Who do I ask for if he doesn't answer the door next time?"

"He will."

"I thought I was a guy you could trust?"

"Hey, man, it's for your own good." Don gulps his Coke, sets it on the table. "I've been thinking. The less you know the better."

"Yeah. I guess. I sure as hell don't want any trouble." I picture the judge's glare, hear Mr. Frogley's warning. "If I end up back in court, I'll get stuck in a group home if I'm lucky. More likely, I'll end up in juvie."

"You worry too much, man." Smiling, he rubs his fingers over the stubble on his chin. "I said I'll keep you out of trouble. Not that I'm expecting a shit-fest or anything. Besides, what could go wrong when no one even knows what you're doing?" He shoves a box full of DVDs out from under the table. "So — you wanna watch a movie?"

"Sure. I guess."

"Hey!" He grabs a DVD. "Remember when your dad took the team to see that baseball movie?"

"No."

"Sure you do. That Kenny kid threw his popcorn up in the air when the little guy finally hit a home run." He laughs.

It all comes flooding back. "*Strike Out.*"

"That's right." Don laughs. "Man, your dad was peeved when everybody copied Kenny."

"Yeah." I chuckle. "All that popcorn flying around."

"And your old man talked the usher into letting us stay."

"Yeah. But then he made us clean up the mess after the show."

Don smiles, shakes his head. "Your dad was a cool dude."

"Yeah." I sit back, stretch my legs out, and put my arms up to cushion the back of my head. Another shiny, prickling memory to play again and again. "That was great."

We end up watching a futuristic action-thriller. Wrapped in my leather seat, munching on warm, salted popcorn, I figure this could be the best movie-going time I've had since *Strike Out*.

So what if I'm not partying; it's great just to be hanging with Don.

Mrs. Ford is so wrong about him.

Still, a little knot tightens in my gut.

Nineteen

Dark clouds pile up across the sky as I head for 23 Braemar the next Saturday.

Skinny comes running before I've gone a block and I break into a jog as he lopes past me. He keeps falling behind or trotting ahead to check out fascinating things like fire hydrants, or a squirrel that does crazy flips and hops across someone's lawn to avoid him. Maybe it's the feel of rain that's got Skinny acting kind of weird.

Eventually, I slow to a walk. I'll probably get drenched. Plus, I can't work outside if it's pouring, so I'll have to come back home and then make some excuse to go out later for the drop off.

I could say I'm going to Nina's to study. Mrs. Ford said she hoped to meet Nina after I told her about the A we got on our geography presentation. It's been ages since I got an A in anything other than math.

I'm chugging up Madill when a guy calls, "Hey! Seb!"

Geoff cuts across the front lawn of a bungalow.

"What're you doing around here, man?" I ask.

"I live here." He nods at the bungalow.

"Really? Donny told me you go to some private school downtown. I figured you lived in a mansion, like him."

"No such luck. Is that skinny mutt yours?"

"No. Not really." Skinny slinks away, as though he doesn't like what Geoff said. Or what I said.

A high voice calls, "Geoff! Geoff! I change my mind."

I look back. The twiggy little kid with a million pigtails from the skate park stands in the doorway to Geoff's house. "Strawberry," she shouts. "Not chocolate. And run! It's going to rain!"

"Okay," Geoff waves. "My sister. I'm going for ice cream while she practices piano."

As we stride up Madill, I say, "I saw her in the skate park once." *As long as my brother doesn't find out.* "Oops. Maybe it wasn't her."

Geoff laughs. "She's not shy, eh? No worries. I don't use the old board anymore. So, what are you doing around here?"

"I live about a mile away. But right now," I say, figuring I can trust Geoff since he knows about the *biz*, "I'm on a mission for Donny — Don. I owe him a favour."

He frowns. "Don't tell me you're going to 23 Braemar."

"How'd you know?"

He snorts. "Been there. Listen man, you seem like a decent guy. Do you really know what you're doing?"

"'Course! Well, maybe." I flash to the first time I went, wondering about the *derelict* driving a cool car. "What do you mean?" I ask.

"Are you in da biz with Don now?" Geoff imitates Sean's voice when he says *da biz*.

"No! I'm just carrying money."

"You hope." He's not smiling.

"Don said he wants to keep me out of trouble." I swallow. "I never actually saw what was in the envelope."

Geoff nods. "He wants to keep himself out of trouble, too. Be careful, man. It could be something other than money."

My jaw stiffens. "Drugs, then?"

"I'm just saying." He shrugs. "Don's pretty smooth. You never really know what's up with him."

"If you think that, why hang out with him?"

Geoff grins. "Why not? It's a rush. Plus, he's got all the toys."

"True." As doubt snakes from my thoughts down to my gut, I force a smile. "And the bruises fade."

Geoff winces. "Oh, yeah. I forgot you got pasted at Burger Kink. I can usually take care of myself."

I work to breathe evenly. Maybe I make this my last pickup.

"We can cut through here," Geoff says as we're passing the skate park. "It might save us getting wet. On the other side of the park, you'll go right: 23 Braemar's real close. And I go left for the corner store."

We're about halfway through the park when three guys climb out of a small car stopped on the far side. They're definitely not boarders, even though two of them wear T-shirts despite the chilly morning. The third one's wearing a cowboy shirt and boots.

Geoff and I slow to a shuffle. The way they're prowling across the park makes me wonder where Skinny's at.

Geoff mutters, "Shit."

The hulk in the middle reminds me of the tanker from Crappy Tire.

The guy to the tanker's right isn't as tall and wears a do-rag like Sean, but there's nothing *wanna-be* about him.

The veins popping from his biceps are big as any of my muscles.

The third guy, stepping around a chipped cement quarter pipe, looks familiar. He's only about five ten or eleven, thin and pale, with a scar across his cheek. Ponytail . . . The hair on my scalp stands up. Carl. The knife.

"So. Here we are," Carl calls, with his soft, high voice. I'd laugh at his cowboy getup and silly swagger, except that my insides have turned to wet cement.

"Where's Don?" he asks.

I shrug.

"Who?" Geoff says.

"You fuckin' stupid?" the guy with the do-rag asks.

I scan the park, the sidewalk. How's it so deserted on a Saturday?

Thunder rumbles the answer.

Carl and his muscles stop on the other side of a low fun box in front of Geoff and me. "So Don's not here," Carl says, shaking his head. "That's too bad."

A little breeze blows goosebumps all over me.

Carl stops his sad act and stares. "What do you think, Jareem?" His face turns toward the guy with the do-rag, but his eyes stay on us. Psycho-Dad all over.

"That's not good," Jareem answers. "How we supposed to communicate, if he don't come to meetings?"

Cold sweat trickles down my neck. I'm praying these guys are going to climb back into their car. Drive away.

The hulk crosses his arms, stares into my eyes. I force myself to meet his stare.

"Well, Jareem, Big T, at least he sent his bitches."

I break eye contact with Big T, force a smile. "Hey man, I don't know what you're talking about, but I'm — "

"But you're what?" His crazy stare shuts me down.

As though on cue, they close in quickly: Big T over the box, Carl and Jareem around opposite sides. My knees want to fold. Jareem is so close, I nearly gag on the sweet stink of his deodorant. No goosebumps on his arms. The hulk plants himself right in front of Geoff.

"But you're what, bitch?" Carl asks again.

"I'm . . . " Dead.

"He's an idiot?" Geoff sounds so cool, it's like he's on tranquilizers.

Carl snickers. "Good one. Still, since Don isn't here," his smile stretches thin, "we'll have to give you ladies the message."

Geoff shuffles his feet.

Carl's right hand slides behind his back.

An electric current sizzles under my skin. Here comes the blade.

Geoff's foot flashes up impossibly high. There's a short, muffled crack. Big T's head jerks back, and he drops to a sit on the fun box. Then Geoff's foot's down and Big T's flat on his back, arms spread wide, legs draped over the edge of the box.

I see my own surprise in the face of Jareem. Then, he's on me. I whip an arm up. Block a punch that drives my wrist into my nose with a sickening crunch. An explosion of pain blinds me.

He grabs my arm, twists it behind my back. Slams my ribs. Something pops, with the sound of a twig snapping.

Gotta get away. Jareem lets go of my arm and his elbow locks around my neck. He yanks my head down, punching. Blood splatters the ground. Another pop.

I swing wildly. My fists, arms crash against rock-hard muscle.

Can't get my breath. He's gonna kill me!

Suddenly, his hold loosens. I twist back, barely keeping my balance. He growls, glances over his shoulder, and kicks out, to the side, missing me. I drive my knee straight into his balls. He grunts, lifts slightly then doubles over, both hands grabbing at his crotch as he falls to his side.

That's when I see Skinny, his teeth latched on to the back of Jareem's ankle. Skinny growled — not Jareem.

"Skin — "

"Seb, look out!"

I stumble backwards. Carl's blade slashes, missing me by a miracle. Geoff's foot collides with Carl's arm. The knife drops and lands beside Big T, who doesn't even twitch.

"Jesus. Fuck!" Carl grabs his arm. "My fucking arm!" He screeches. "You broke my fucking arm! Jareem!" With his left hand, he holds his right hand out in front of him. His forearm sags like putty above the wrist.

Jareem doesn't even look. He's holding himself and moaning. His leg twitches. Skinny's still attached.

Trying to catch my breath, I manage, "Good boy, Skinny."

Carl gives Geoff a frightened look then kicks Big T in the shin. "Wake the fuck up!"

Geoff grabs my shoulder. "Holy shit. You okay?"

"Yeah! I'm good. Thought he was gonna kill me. Actually, I'm really good, considering — "

Geoff shakes his head. "You're punked, man. Come on. Let's get out of here." He glances at Carl and Jareem.

Big T is still out. Carl gives him another kick. "Wake up!"

I can't seem to get myself together. Can't get my buttons done up. "Hey — where'd the buttons go?"

"Seb, forget about the stupid jacket!" Geoff yanks my arm. "Come on!"

Thunder crashes overhead.

I trip over a mini pipe, lurch around a flattop. Follow Geoff out of the park. Pellets of rain slice down. I can barely feel them. Barely feel anything.

Crossing the street, I look back through the downpour. Carl stands on top of the box now, rain-soaked shirt plastered to his back. His voice whines through the storm. "Come on you guys. You gotta take me to the fuckin' hospital. Get up!" Holding his arm, he pushes a pointed toe under Big T, who starts to sit up. Skinny's still latched onto Jareem.

A police siren sounds.

"I can't be here, Geoff."

Geoff grabs my ripped coat. "So, let's go!" He pulls me along the sidewalk.

"Skinny. Here boy!" I focus on getting one foot in front of the other. Glance back as Skinny skitters across the street behind me.

Geoff says, "Thought he wasn't your dog."

Twenty

I'm cold, I taste blood, and I'm barely able to stand. But I'm alive.

Geoff props me against a post on his big back porch. "Stay right here. I'll be out in a second. Shanisse!" He bounds through the back door.

I close my eyes. Focus on staying vertical. The rain slows.

"Hi there." Geoff's little sister drags a kitchen chair out the door. Her face is scrunched up, like I smell bad. "I'm Shanisse." She holds a finger to her lips. "We already met," she whispers.

I nod. "I'm Seb."

She scrapes the chair across the porch, past a couch I could sure use. "We don't want yucky blood stains on our good, old sofa."

"I figured," I mumble.

"So, you sit here, Seb."

I hold the porch railing and ease myself onto the chair.

"You're sure wet." She darts back into the house.

Skinny leaps onto the porch, shakes, and then curls up tight, so that most of him fits between the legs of my chair.

Shannise reappears with a towel. "Hey! Is that dog yours?"

"No — " He saved my life. "I mean, I guess so."

Shanisse wraps the towel around my shoulders.

"Thanks."

Geoff comes out with a handful of white stuff, a roll of paper towel, and a big bowl of water. A few minutes later, my nose is completely stuffed with cotton balls.

"Your nose is definitely busted," Geoff says.

I touch it with shaky fingers. Least it's still there, pointing the right way. "Thanks for bringing me here, Geoff."

He smiles. "I was afraid I might need the wheelbarrow."

I try to laugh. Pain rips through my chest.

"What's wrong?" Geoff asks.

"Even breathing hurts."

"The way he whaled on you, I bet you've got broken ribs." He hands me a wad of wet paper towel and turns to Shanisse, who's holding the bowl of water. "Can you help Seb get cleaned up while I go find tape for his cuts?"

Shanisse frowns. "No?"

"All you need to do is point on your face where Seb should wipe blood off his."

"Oh! I can do that. I'll be like the talking *mirror mirror on the wall* who tells Snow White's stepmother *who's the fair —* "

"Just point! I'll be right back."

"Okay." Shanisse lowers the bowl to the porch floor then sits beside it. "Here we go, Seb." She touches a spot on her chin. "And here." She rubs under her nose. "A bit more blood leaked out." She points at her eyebrow. "I'm going to be a doctor someday." She brushes her cheek. "Your mom is going to kill you."

"No, she's not." But what about Mrs. Ford? Second screw-up in less than two months. If she finds out why I was beaten up, she'll call CSC. I'll end up in Hassles' group home. I sigh. Pain tears through me again. Idiot.

"My mom would kill me, and she's going to kill Geoff when she finds out he was in another fight."

"She finds out and you won't make it to eleven. Got that, Shanisse?" Geoff says, coming out with tape and scissors.

"If she asks, I can't lie." Shanisse's eyes fill her face. She'd rather piss off her brother than her mother.

"She won't ask, unless you say something stupid."

As Geoff tapes a couple cuts above my eyes, Shanisse talks nonstop. "Our mom says if you know someone, you can tell when they're lying."

"Oh?"

"Yeah. Mom says you always do the same thing — like blink or play with your hair — when you're lying."

"You do that?" I ask.

She shakes her head. "I don't lie. Your dog's not very friendly."

I go to pet Skinny, who's still under my chair, but remember I can't bend that far without killing myself. "He's friendly."

"Then maybe he's just tired," Shanisse says. "Hey! I've got a joke. You know how people say dogs are their best friends?"

I nod.

"Because you have to know that to get this joke."

"Okay."

Geoff tapes a cut above my ear.

"So, here's the joke: Outside of a dog, a book is a girl's best friend. Inside of a dog, it's too dark to read. Get it?" She laughs. "Like, in a dog's stomach — "

"You need to practice your delivery, Shanisse." Geoff gives one of her pigtails a little tug. "I kept expecting the cops to show," he says. "I guess it was the thunder that finally got someone to look out their window."

"I wasn't thinking about the cops. Wasn't thinking anything except that Jareem was gonna kill me. My body just took over."

"Adrenalin, man."

"Did you like the joke?" Shanisse starts pointing for me again. "Still some blood there."

I nod.

Geoff hands me more wet paper. "For your hands."

My knuckles are scraped and bleeding. "I never kneed a guy before. Sissy move. Don't feel bad about it, though."

Geoff snorts. "He had it coming."

Shanisse says, "I never needed a guy either. But that reminds me: where's my ice cream, Geoff?"

Geoff scowls. "Shanisse!" He takes my bloody paper towels, drops them into a plastic bag. "Try to straighten up. That'll help your ribs."

I press my back against the chair. "I couldn't believe it when you took out Big T."

Shanisse sits straighter. "My brother got his black belt in tae kwon do three times already."

"Lucky thing."

"I've got my orange belt." Shanisse smiles. "I can teach you some punches and kicks, Seb."

"If you're interested, I could, too." Geoff leans over, pulls another of Shanisse's pigtails. "How about getting Seb and me a drink?"

Her eyes go huge again. "You mean, beer?" She giggles.

"No, silly. Not beer. Orange juice. Please?"

After she goes inside, Geoff plunks down on the top step. "So, what do you think, man?"

"About what?"

"About what went down there. About Don." He watches me, one eyebrow raised.

Then I get it. "You think he set us up?"

"Us?" He shakes his head. "You were just freaking lucky I showed up, man."

I force myself to focus. Nobody but Mrs. Ford and Mr. Frogley knew I'd be at Fairhaven. So meeting Geoff really was pure luck. And nobody but Donny knew I'd be going to 23 Braemar.

"You think he set *me* up! Me instead of him?" For an instant, the only pain I can feel is my chest caving. I close my eyes, *breathe, one, two, three, four* . . . I take shallow breaths, try to think. "No. Wait! You're wrong."

Geoff tilts his head.

"I didn't even know I'd be in the skate park. So, Don couldn't have known."

"I don't know." He shrugs. "I'm not sure about anything. I guess it could've been a coincidence. It's just — those guys were parked on Braemar. If you've always gone the long way around to 23, you wouldn't have seen that the park goes over there, too. You've gotta wonder."

Wish I could stop shivering.

"Carl could've been watching the house and happened to see us," Geoff says. "He would have recognized us from Burger Kink. Anyhow, don't sweat it, Seb. There's no point. At least, not now. Now, we gotta get you home."

I shake my head.

"I'm going to call a cab. My mom can't see you and you're not walking."

"No. I can't let Mrs. Ford see me."

"Mrs. Ford? You don't live with your mom?"

I shake my head. "Foster parent. She'll call the cops. That can't happen."

"Listen, Seb. Just don't tell anyone you recognized any of those guys. Got that? Give me Ford's number. I'll talk to her before you get there so she doesn't freak. Don't worry, man."

I give him the phone number. "Tell her . . . " Pain spins through my brain. "It happened on my way to work."

Shanisse comes out holding a glass of juice in each hand. "Sorry I was so slow," she says, glaring at Geoff. "I had to mix up a whole new batch because someone hogged the last one."

"Sorry." Geoff puffs his lips out and Shanisse laughs.

The taxi barely splashes to a stop before Mrs. Ford opens its back door. One look at me and her face shrivels. She closes her umbrella. "We're going to St. Joe's," she tells the driver.

"No! Wait! I'll be fine. It looks worse than it feels," I lie and stretch one foot out of the cab.

"You need to be checked out by a doctor."

"I'm not going to a hospital." What if Carl's there? What if the doctor calls the cops?

"Your friend said you may have some broken ribs. Stay right there." She lifts my foot gently back into the cab, then closes my door and hops into the front seat. "St. Joe's, please." During the short drive there, she says, "Geoff told me what happened."

In the Emergency waiting room, as I tell her how Skinny helped me, I glance at everyone coming and going before I realize that Carl probably went to hospital — this or some other — while I was at Geoff's.

It's not long before I'm being peered at, prodded, and asked a bunch of questions behind a flimsy curtain. The doctor wants to know if I was knocked out, if I'm dizzy, and, on a scale of one to ten, how much pain I feel.

When he's finished, he asks Mrs. Ford to step inside my little curtained cubicle. "Sebastian's lucky he stayed on his feet. He's got a couple of cracked ribs which he'll feel for a few months, but besides prescribing pain killers, we don't do anything for that. His nose should heal pretty well. Just keep the bandage on four or five days. You said you're a nurse, right?"

Mrs. Ford nods.

"I don't think you'll see any signs of internal bleeding, but just in case, keep an eye on him for the next — " He glances at his notes. "Five hours or so."

Mrs. Ford nods again. "Any bloating, I'll get him back here immediately."

The doctor is almost ready to leave when Mrs. Ford says, "Sebastian was attacked because he was mistaken for someone else. I think the police should be involved, don't you, Doctor?"

I stifle a groan, pray, *Please, no.*

159

"Did you know these guys?" the doctor asks me. "Ever seen them before?"

I shake my head.

"That's too bad." His raised eyebrows say he's not buying my lie. He scribbles a prescription and hands it to Mrs. Ford. "Tylenol 3. We're obliged to call in the police when presented with knife or gun wounds. Otherwise, they're not getting involved."

I breathe a small sigh of relief.

Mrs. Ford fills the prescription at the hospital pharmacy, gives me a couple painkillers, and I practically crawl into a cab to head home.

Sitting in the front again, Mrs. Ford looks back at me. "Did those thugs give you any clue — other than the wrong name — *why*, Seb?"

I shake my head.

"You know I have to inform Ms. Haslett."

"Please, Mrs. Ford." My voice catches in my throat. "I'm going to talk to someone. Some guy who maybe knows who beat me up. Okay? Let me try to figure it out. Please."

"I don't like being lied to." Mrs. Ford's stare isn't cutting like the judge's, but it puts a knot in my gut.

"I don't like being lied to either." But I'm too dead to think about Donny anymore right now.

Back home, as I drag myself out of the taxi, Mrs. Ford holds an open umbrella over me. She gasps. "Look! This must be Skinny."

Skinny races at us, jumps up to lick my face, and then wriggles in a fit of happiness.

I laugh for a moment before pain throbs through my ribs. "That's a first."

"He's obviously been waiting for you," Mrs. Ford says. "That's devotion."

I rub his wet head — all I can reach without bending too far.

The taxi takes off and Mrs. Ford says, "Let's get you into the house, Seb."

Skinny backs away, tail down.

I'm about to beg Mrs. Ford to let him in the house just this once when she says, "Don't you worry, Skinny. We won't leave you out in the rain. I think my old Trixie's bed is still somewhere in there."

"He can stay?" I forget about my ribs, breathing so deep that, despite the painkiller, it feels as though my chest might split open.

"You're quite sure he has no owner, right?" Mrs. Ford smiles. "I think he deserves a better home than the street."

I blink in amazement.

Then, on top of every other ache, that guilty knot jabs at my gut again. If she's letting Skinny stay, she must be letting me stay. She deserves the truth — about Don, about everything.

I'll tell her. But later. When I'm feeling better.

Twenty-One

Sunday evening, I sit on the couch straight as I can so my ribs won't ache, and try to stop thinking about whether Donny somehow set me up.

Mrs. Ford is about to turn on the TV for us when the doorbell rings, so she goes for that instead.

"You've got a visitor, Seb," she says a minute later. "And I just remembered, Skinny's probably finished outside." She heads for the back door and Geoff walks into the living room. He's carrying a tin in one hand.

I nod. "Hey."

He takes one look at the dark bruises that cover over half my face now and his eyes bulge. "Whoa!" He rocks backward and shouts, "Frankenstein." Then he blinks, and shakes his head. "Di-did I just say that out loud?"

I laugh for a moment. My ribs scream. I slap my arms around my chest. "Don't do that, man!"

He hands me the tin. "Shanisse made cookies for you."

I pull off the lid. "Little bunches of grapes?"

He looks. "They're *supposed* to be four-leaf clovers. I guess I busted 'em. Too bad," he whispers. "Now it'll be like you're eating a lot of tiny green guys' junk."

I snort, forgetting my ribs again. "Don't make me laugh!"

162

Skinny trots into the living room, sniffs Geoff's legs, then lies down at my feet.

Mrs. Ford peers in from the hall. "I'm going downstairs to do some ironing, so I'll say goodbye now, Geoff, in case I don't get a chance to later. I hope I'll see you again."

Geoff smiles. "I hope so, too."

"I told Don what happened," he says once Mrs. Ford is out of earshot.

"What did he say? Was he surprised?"

Geoff shrugs. "He may have been, but he didn't show it. He said, *Carl's one scary little psycho.*"

"That's it?" Not even, *Poor Seb?*

"No." Geoff frowns at Shanisse's cookies for a bit then looks back at me, and suddenly I don't want to hear anymore. "He said, *I guess it really does suck to be Sebastian.*"

The air leaves my lungs as though Rose's lineman just kicked me again. I can't look Geoff in the eye.

"Maybe he felt bad for you. But, you need to know where you stand," he says. "He only wants *me* around when he expects trouble."

I remember Donny all stoked about Geoff's *kung fu thing.*

"You should really take it up with him, man," he says.

I nod. "Except, I don't think he meant for me to get pounded." And I like being Don's *old pal from back in the day.* He probably doesn't really think I'm pathetic.

Geoff spends most of the next ten minutes trying to make me laugh. When he does, my ribs hurt so much I beg him to stop.

"Like I said yesterday," he says when he's about to leave. "I don't mind helping you with some tae kwon do moves, if you're down with that. You're coordinated. And it's a great discipline, even if you never really need it again."

I figure somehow he sees from the bruises that I don't want any more fights. "Thanks. When I'm feeling solid again."

"Okay. Later, bro."

After Geoff lets himself out, I pat the couch and Skinny hops up beside me. "Geoff's a good guy, eh?" I scratch behind Skinny's ears. "Don probably does use him, but that doesn't mean he uses everyone." Skinny stretches out and lays his head in my lap. "Don said he's keeping me out of things for my own good." I'll talk to him, but that had to be some weird coincidence in the skate park.

Wednesday I'm back at school with black eyes, a bandage on my nose, and ribs that hurt if I cough, sneeze, laugh, yawn, burp, bend . . . do pretty much anything.

When Nina rushes up to me on the way into our first class, she nearly drops her books. "What the heck? You got a nose job? Why? I like big noses. They run in my family. No pun intended."

We're early, but a few more kids file in behind us.

I ease myself onto my chair. "I did not get a nose job. I — "

"You mean the old one's still under the tape? That's a relief." She sits at the desk across the aisle from me.

"Thanks."

Even though there are other conversations going on around us, I'm glad she's lowered her voice. "So, did you walk into a glass wall or something?" she asks, arranging everything she needs for Math — from her calculator to her fake rabbit's foot — beside her workbook.

"Or something." I don't want to share the truth with Nina any more than I want to share it with Mrs. Ford or Mr. Frogley.

"Hey!" She frowns. "This had something to do with that stolen bike — right?"

I shrug. How does she figure things so quickly?

"I knew it! Did Don punch you?" She talks fast and low. "No. He wouldn't do that. Did he ask you to lean on someone and they beat you up? What?"

I don't answer, just try to keep my breathing shallow so my ribs don't hurt.

"Well, I've been waiting to show you this." She whips a piece of paper from a binder and holds it up just long enough for me to see it's full of strange names and places. "I was doing research for my college education, because next year I'll be applying for all the financial help I can get. And," she says, reaching to drop the sheet on my desk, "I thought this info might excite *you*." She stabs a finger at the top of the page: *Scholarships, Bursaries, and Awards for Seb.* "They're for *Math*." Her eyes narrow. "But you can't stay away from trouble, so what was I thinking?" Her whisper has turned into more of a hiss. "You could probably have your whole college education paid for, if you weren't stupidly getting stoned and fighting and — "

Ms. Burk rushes into the room, grabs an eraser to clean the blackboard, as always, and then sees me. "Seb, may I speak with you for a moment?"

"Sure." My left ear is burning. I push myself up and away from Nina as fast as I can.

165

When I get to the front, Ms. Burk blinks and presses her lips together so tight her bright red lipstick completely disappears. She seems to be in more pain just looking at me than I am.

"The office let your teachers know what Mrs. Ford reported," she says quietly. "So how are you doing now?"

"Doing okay, thanks. Just gotta catch up on the homework, I guess."

The lip press turns into a little smile. "That's the spirit. I'll have that ready for you at the end of class. Let's hope something like this never happens again."

No kidding, I think as she pats my arm and gives me the pained lip press again.

I head back to my seat, everyone in the class gawking at me except Nina. She's staring at her textbook and doesn't even glance my way.

The *Scholarships, Bursaries, and Awards for Seb* sheet is still lying on my desk. I shove it into my pants pocket. Then I spend the rest of the period trying to pay attention to Ms. Burk and wondering how much of an idiot I really am.

At lunch, I avoid Nina and Matt, and make a weak attempt to find Don. I end up eating alone, sitting on the boulder at the edge of the pine trees. It's a nice break from the weird looks, questions, and razzing I've been getting all morning.

When I'm almost finished eating, I pull out Nina's info sheet and press the creases out of it. After studying it for a minute, it makes sense. The different amounts of money are offered by different schools. Nina's even included web addresses for everything.

I head back to school thinking about doing more research into it on my own. Amazingly, I'm feeling no pain.

At three forty-five Nina leans against my locker, her packed knapsack and violin case on the floor beside her. And she once called *me* a stalker.

"Thanks for that bursary and scholarship information," I say. "Can I please get into my locker?"

She moves out of my way. "So who beat you up? And why?" She doesn't sound like she's spitting mad anymore.

I sigh, which hurts. "Some guy I've never seen before. And I'm not sure why."

"But you were doing Don a favour, right? Half the kids in this school know what that means: you were selling drugs for him."

"I wasn't." I chuck a couple textbooks into the locker. "He asked me to collect some cash and I got beaten up on the way there."

"That's weird. Why wouldn't the guy have jumped you afterwards to get the money?"

"It was pretty random."

"You better be careful, Seb, you never know — it could happen again."

"Don't worry. It won't."

A few minutes later, as Nina and I cut through the parking lot, I spot Don ducking into the forest. "Sorry, Nina, but I gotta talk to him. Find out what gives."

"Are you crazy?" she practically shouts. "The guy's a snake."

"I'm going."

"Okay." She puts down her violin. "I'll wait here."

"No. I'll see you tomorrow."

167

Just days ago, I would have said Nina didn't know what she was talking about, but now I don't know what to think. I head for the trees, taking a deep breath that nearly ruptures my ribs.

⟋

"Listen, man. I had no clue." Don sits on his favourite log, smoking a joint. "Honestly!" He rubs his jaw.

"So, why were they there?" I ask, careful to keep my breathing shallow.

He hesitates. "How should I know? Sit!" He slides over. "Have a toke!"

"No thanks." I work to keep my voice steady. "It couldn't have been a coincidence. They asked for you."

He tilts his head and studies the joint. "This shit's supposed to calm me down. Anyway, Sebastian." He tries to toke, but it's gone out. "Here's the truth."

I hold my breath.

"Carl thinks I ripped him off. I don't know why, because I didn't. I wouldn't." He scratches his stubbly chin and then flicks the lighter. Nothing happens, so he shakes it. "Anyhow, the guy on Braemar can be a real whore. I thought he might tell Carl I'd be by."

"So, you knew Carl would be there!" Rage simmers through me.

"No! I thought Carl *might* be there and *if* he was he'd want to get even. But . . . "

"*Get even?*"

Don glances toward the street.

"What for?" I ask through clenched teeth. "If you didn't rip him off."

Don tries the lighter again. It flames. "You know what I mean, Sebastian." He takes another toke. "He thinks I did. And I thought, even if he showed, he'd leave you alone. After all," he grins, "you're not me."

I feel like I'm shrinking.

Don stands, knuckle-punches my shoulder. "But you're okay. Just some bruises now, eh?" He holds out the joint.

I shake my head. "And cracked ribs."

"So after a few more pickups on Braemar, we're all square."

"What?" But I heard him. I can barely breathe. He better be kidding.

"A couple." He blows a smoke ring. "Pretty good, eh?"

I swallow. "I gotta go."

"So, next Saturday, Sebastian?"

"No way. I'm done." I head back toward the street. My legs feel like they're made of cement.

"Sebastian," Donny says. "What the hell? We'll figure something else out."

My chest throbs. I try to stand straight, and keep walking.

So, maybe it wasn't a set-up. But, who knows?

No more doobies with Donny. No more nothin'. I'm never gonna owe him again.

Twenty-Two

"**D**on't you just love how dogs say hello to each other?" Nina asks.

The corridor is full of people rushing to get a head start on Friday evening.

To avoid one of Nina's lectures on not doing enough homework, I pull some books out of my locker. "Sure. You mean, how they sniff each other?" She doesn't have to know I probably won't open my knapsack all weekend.

"Yeah," she says, packing nearly everything she owns. "No small talk, chit-chat, bullshit for them. Within seconds of sticking their noses in each other's butts, they know what we humans could spend months discovering. Like, each other's mood, health, age, attitude, sexual bent."

"Guess you really like working at the shelter, eh?"

"Yep." She closes her backpack. "Your ear's red again, Seb. You okay?"

I nod.

"Golden retrievers are prone to ear infections. But you're more of a Great Dane."

I laugh.

She heaves her pack onto her back then wraps her arms around four binders.

"Want me to carry a couple of those?" I ask.

"Sure! Does that mean your ribs are all better?"

"They're getting there."

I'm shoving her binders into my bag when I hear, "Sebastian!"

Don powers through the crowd like a pit bull on a mission. I've been staying away from him for the last few weeks, but there's no avoiding him now. He brushes past Nina, stops in front of me.

"Hey, Don." A tug at my gut reminds me I still haven't come clean with Mrs. Ford about everything.

"Sebastian, my man." He sounds cheerful. Nina raises her eyebrows before opening a binder and pretending to read.

Don plants his hand high on the locker beside mine. His rumble-ready rings flash.

I shuffle backwards, but my locker door's there.

Don leans in. "You know those guys . . . ," he lowers his voice, " . . . who gave you a rough time?"

I nod. Get a whiff of his rotten pit. He glances up and down the hall. Looks back at me. "Me and the boys are going to cut them some new ones tonight."

"Oh?" If I were a foot shorter, I'd duck into my locker, close the door right now.

"You remember the Fairhaven field? We played some games there?"

I nod again, amazed at the coincidence. But I'm sure I never told him about Mr. Frogley or Fairhaven. So that's what it must be — coincidence.

"Be there! Seven thirty. This is your chance to give back."

"I can't." A bead of sweat seeps down the side of my face. Will Mr. Frogley still be there? He's not usually that late. I don't want him getting mixed up with Don's plan.

"Bullshit. Come on, man." His eyes narrow. "We need you. Kung fu boy fucked off. The guy's really a wuss."

Trying to stay cool, I say, "Maybe Geoff's got better things to do. And, you can get even for me, 'cause I'm busy, too."

"Oh? What are you so *busy* with?"

My mind races. Mrs. Ford? Not. Leaving town? Party? He won't believe any of it. I feel like I'm in a tiny, stinking jail cell.

"You never did make it up for that bike, Sebastian. You were supposed — "

"I think I did." My eyeballs feel as though they're vibrating. "But I'll buy you a lousy bike if I have to."

His smile twitches. "Hey! I told you, I had no clue they would show! Come on, I've seen you kick ass."

Nina catches my eye, jerks her head, as in *let's go!* Inspiration hits. "Anyhow, I've got a date."

Nina's eyes open wide. *Who?* she mouths.

Don snorts. "You are so fucking full of it."

Keep it together, Seb. I shrug — my answer for Nina and Don.

Don drops the smile, shoves his face up to mine. "So, who's your date?"

Now I'm breathing his sour cigarette breath. More sweat slides down my neck.

He pokes me in the chest. "You're a lying. Little. Chickenshit. Coward."

The hard edge of my open locker presses into my back. A fire starts burning in my chest, spreads up my neck, flows into my arms. "I said, I'm busy."

Nina slams her binder shut. "Let's go, Lover! I've got things to do before the movie."

Don whips around to look at her. Misses me nearly tip over from shock. When he turns back, I bluff: tilt my head, lift a shoulder, as if to say, *Told you so.*

His face twists into a scowl. "Skinny fucking faggot." He punches my shoulder then strides away.

"You okay?" Nina's voice is a whisper.

I nod. "Nina, thanks . . . "

She lifts a hand. "Don't mention it. But you owe me. Big time." She winks. "Let's go."

My hands are shaking as I tug my knapsack on. I feel like I used to after an evening of dodging Dad-A-Dick's fiery attacks.

We're past the forest when Nina says, "Matt thinks that things usually balance."

"Hmm?" I can't stop thinking about Don and his stinkin' plans. I don't buy his revenge line. Perhaps this is some kind of turf war.

"I mean, Don's tough-guy act. All that bullying, fuckity-fuck-fuck-fuck, *you're a chicken*-type talk. He's probably got a wickedly insecure side to him. You know — yin and yang."

"Maybe." Mr. Frogley and I should be long gone before there's any trouble at Fairhaven. Still, a nervous buzz makes my muscles tense. Why? This is not my problem.

A couple of blocks later, Nina asks, "Seb, when did Don see you *kick ass*? Were you in another fight?"

"Yes. But it wasn't planned. And I didn't kick anyone's ass."

"When was that?"

"Too many questions."

"But — "

I sigh. "Listen, Nina. I'm not going to fight, okay? I wouldn't go even if it didn't still hurt to cough. Besides, if Mrs. Ford found out, I could end up in a lot of trouble."

"Who's Mrs. Ford?"

Her question catches me by surprise. "My foster mom."

"Are you kidding me?" She stops walking. "You couldn't have mentioned that?"

I don't slow. "It's not my favourite topic."

"Seb, I'm sorry." She hurries to catch up. "I mean, about you being fostered. And that you didn't think you could tell me. Do you always keep that secret?"

I shrug. "Most people either ask a lot of questions, which I hate, or they steer clear of me once they know." Suddenly I recall telling Don stuff about being fostered that first time we smoked in the forest. "But, Don was cool about it." Maybe he's been telling the truth all along.

"Go figure." Nina shakes her head. "Anyhow, I won't ask you what happened. At least not now." She doesn't wink. "But I'm not ditching you, either. Geez."

After a bit, when I don't say anything, Nina says, "Okay — forget the Great Dane. You're more of a lone wolf."

Huh! That's cool. I smile. "Mrs. Ford seems okay. I meant to tell you she was pretty excited about all that Math award and scholarship stuff." Especially the ones Ms. Burk had agreed I'd be sure to get if I just kept on doing my thing.

"Oh my gosh! When I gave you that information, I didn't even know . . . " Nina looks up at me — speechless, for once.

"And did I mention she let Skinny move in?" I ask.

"Oh? No, you didn't." She sounds a little pissed. "But, that's great. So, obviously you're not bringing him to the shelter."

"Huh?"

"Yeesh. I knew you weren't listening that time I said we could find him a home. Hey, there he is."

Skinny high steps around me, wagging his tail.

"Hey, boy." I pet him. He turns to Nina, sniffing.

She laughs. "Wonder what he'll learn sniffing *my* butt!"

I groan.

~

After dropping Nina's stuff at her place, I jog home, my injured ribs still jolting with each step. I grab a snack for me and a handful of treats for Skinny, then head out to Fairhaven. Trotting beside me, Skinny looks happier, though not much heavier, than when we first met.

I can't stop wondering about Don. "Why's he fighting Carl and those guys, eh Skinny? It can't really be about me, can it? It's gotta be the drugs."

I've got a queasy feeling in my gut. I stop to take a bunch of slow and careful breaths, bent so that my hands press against my knees for support. Skinny nudges my thigh with his nose.

"I'm okay, boy." So, why the storm inside?

Because random shit happens. Because I'm sick of getting swept up into one pile of garbage after another.

175

Because I don't want Mr. Frogley to know about me and Don.

Skinny licks my cheek and I straighten. "How often have Mr. Frogley and I been at the school after seven, Skinny? Hardly ever. We'll be finished before anyone shows up."

By the time I reach Fairhaven I'm covered in sweat. Mr. Frogley takes one look. "What's wrong? You sick?"

"No." I clear my throat. "Just hot from running."

"Well, come on, then. It's all inside today. Lots to do for some special conference tomorrow. Got to get the place shining, set up chairs in the gym . . . "

I leave Skinny checking out the dumpster, as usual.

As we sweep our piles of sawdust along the hall, I check my watch. We should be out of here by six thirty No sweat.

I'm almost at the end of the hall when Mr. Frogley calls, "You must have some big plans for tonight."

I'm way ahead of him now. Guess I have been working a little faster, just to be safe.

He laughs. "I'll have to start calling you Hercules! You know he had red hair, too, eh?"

I force a laugh. Glance at my watch.

Two piss-stinking toilets need unclogging. After that, I swab the bathroom floor. It's six twenty-seven when I figure we're done.

As we put the mops back in his office, Mr. Frogley says, "One last job."

"Another one?"

He smiles. "You really are in a rush tonight, aren't you? You got a hot date planned?"

I shrug.

Maybe I should tell him. No. I already said I didn't know who beat me up. Said I was in the wrong place at the wrong time. Which is true. Just not the whole truth. I'm not telling any more lies. At least not to Mr. Frogley. "So, what are we doing?"

"We have to clean the windows in all the doors."

I must look how I feel, because Mr. Frogley says, "Don't you worry about it. You want to leave, go ahead. I'll get it done in no time."

"No." I sure don't want him here alone. "I'll help."

Mr. Frogley pulls Windex and a couple squeegees off a shelf above his desk. At the side door, he demonstrates how the job's done. "Don't leave streaks. They look even worse when the sun's shining."

Six thirty-five. This shouldn't take more than twenty, thirty minutes.

I work so fast, my shoulder's sore when we finish at seven ten. Mr. Frogley locks up and we head out to the parking lot.

"Can I give you a lift tonight?"

The sky is grey. It'll be dark soon. I glance at my watch. Seven fifteen. What if the guys show early? What if Donny sees me? Every nerve in my body screams, *run*. "Is it okay if Skinny comes with me?"

"Yes, sir." He unlocks the car.

I whistle for Skinny. He doesn't appear. That means he'll meet up with me somewhere on the way home. "Thanks, anyway. But I guess I better walk." Seven seventeen.

"Okay, Seb. Thanks for the help this evening."

I don't say anything. Just nod.

"You're a good worker."

177

I can barely stand still. Let's go!

"The union can be a tricky business, but I bet I could get you a part-time job in a non-union shop that pays pretty good, now you're just about finished your court hours. How's that sound?"

I can't think. "Good. Sounds good." Stop myself from looking at my watch. "But, I should get going."

"Sorry, Seb. Here I am blabbing away when you're in a rush. You go on. We'll talk about the job next week." He tucks into the car. "Have a real good evening!"

"Thanks." I glance at the time. Seven twenty.

I'm striding out of the driveway when Mr. Frogley's Chevy rattles past. He tips his hat. I wave, relieved to see him leave.

Who cares what happens there now? Not my problem.

Mr. Frogley probably thinks I'm a jerk. Shrugging at a great job offer, rushing off. What's Skinny up to? I stop, pull a dog treat from my pocket, and call, "Skinny."

Still no sign of him. I whistle. Maybe he got a date. Something better than a piece of dried liver. I pocket the treat. Seven thirty-five.

I'm at the bottom of Madill when I hear a siren wailing somewhere behind me. I turn and catch a police cruiser flashing through the T-stop at the top of the street going opposite the way I just came.

Coincidence. It can't be going to the school now. Can it? Seven fifty.

Another siren blares. A second cruiser and an ambulance fly through the intersection.

My heart's racing as though the sirens are coming for me.

But they're not.

And even if they're going to Fairhaven, it's not my problem.

I scan Madill. The sky, grass, everything's grey. "Skinny. Here, boy."

Mr. Frogley and I did our cleanup. We . . . the chairs. We forgot to set up the chairs. Mr. Frogley probably went back.

My heart pounds in my ears.

Racing up Madill, a cramp in my side slows me down. I couldn't get away fast enough. Now all I want is to get back.

It's dark when I pass a small bunch of people gathered at the edge of the school property. Gawkers. "Hey! Watch out!" a woman calls.

The red and blue lights of a cop car make creepy reflections in the school's front windows. Goosebumps bristle over my scalp before I even spot Mr. Frogley's car.

I'm running through the parking lot, heading for the side doors. Suddenly, a policeman is in front of me. "Stop. You can't go back there."

"I have to. My friend's here." I don't sound like me. My voice is jagged. "He might be in the school. Or out there." I point. "In the field."

"Slow down, kid."

"I gotta go see!" I stop myself from pushing the cop out of my way.

"Well, you can't." A walkie-talkie-type thing attached to the cop's vest splutters. He pushes a button on it, says, "It's on the way."

Twenty-Three

M r. Frogley's been hurt. I know it. My fault. I should have warned him. "Where is he? I've gotta see him."

"Hold on." The cop motions to someone behind me.

A second ambulance rolls up, lights flashing, but no siren. "I'm gonna go help him now. Okay?" I say.

The cop ignores me.

The driver sticks his head out the window. "They on the field?"

They? Who else got hurt? Don? Carl?

The cop points. "Asphalt. Turn left."

The ambulance shoots forward. I take off, charging after it. I half expect to be tackled, but nothing happens, except the cop yells, "Hey."

I scramble around back of the school. Another ambulance and three more police cruisers are parked on the asphalt beside the field. Together, they make a sort of semicircle, some facing in, some out. Two spotlights on the school wall and all the headlights cut through the dark. The back doors of the ambulance I was chasing are already open.

Where is everybody? My pace slows. Almost everyone is a cop; they're over by the ambulances, walking between the cruisers. I figured there'd be ten, twenty guys. But no. There's nobody I know.

Jogging closer, I spot Mr. Frogley on a stretcher. I race to his side.

His eyes are open, scared. There's a plastic mask over his nose and mouth. I don't see any blood.

"Mr. Frogley," is all I can get out as two guys with glow-tape vests carry him past.

The one at Mr. Frogley's feet says, "Out of the way!"

Mr. Frogley whispers, "Seb. I'm sorry."

"*You're* sorry?"

He closes his eyes.

"What happened?"

The same stretcher guy says, "Probably a heart attack."

The other guy says, "You want to help him? Don't make him talk."

They slide him into the second ambulance.

"Where are you taking him?" My teeth are chattering.

"St. Joseph's."

"Can I go?"

"Not with us."

"You're going to be okay, Mr. Frogley," I call as the doors slam shut.

Please don't die.

The ambulance races around the corner, its siren blaring.

Two beams of light sweep back and forth out in the field. I can barely make out the people attached to the small end of each shaft, but they've got that cop look, too.

I'm wondering what they'll find in Sin Central when I notice no one's hanging around the back of the other ambulance now. I take a few steps, so that I can see who's inside.

It's Sean, his face white as the padding on the wall he's sitting beside.

I edge closer, wondering what's wrong. "Hey! Sean." Soon as I say it I could kick myself. Now Don will know I lied.

But Sean stares out unblinking, like a zombie. He doesn't seem to notice me. A woman all in black turns around in the far corner. I gasp, wonder how *I* didn't notice *her*. She glances at me then bends over Sean and pushes his shoulders so that he lies down.

Maybe he won't tell Don I was here.

A cop heads over so I step away. The cop talks to the paramedic for a couple of minutes then closes the doors, thumps the side, and the ambulance rolls away.

I trail after the cop, working up the nerve to ask for a ride to the hospital. This weird feeling, like the air's thicker or heavier, slides over me and suddenly I know I'm being watched.

I glance at a cruiser parked just to my left and, with the weird light and reflections, see a creepy mix of eyes, bricks, and teeth in a backseat window. Somebody's staring out at me. Smiling.

"How's your dog?" Jareem calls through the glass.

My knees disappear. I have to tell myself I'm safe — he can't get me from a cop car. "What do you care?" I shake off a prickly feeling.

The cop turns around. "You know him?" He jerks his head toward Jareem.

My whole body's trembling. I can barely think. I manage one deep breath.

The cop's eyebrows twitch. "Hmm?"

"No. I've just seen him around." Shit. I can't get mixed up in this. "I came to help Mr. Frogley, the man who had a heart attack." If I keep talking, he won't get a chance to. "I work with him. Here. Fairhaven. He's the janitor. I just got here. Ask the cop — er, police officer — out front." Wish Jareem wasn't there, listening to me babble. "He told me Mr. Frogley was back here."

"That so?" The cop squints at me. His tough-guy act doesn't match his baby face. "So, what do you know about what went on here?"

"Nothing." Too quick. Sounds like I'm lying again. "Except my boss had a heart attack. And he's going to the hospital."

"Okay. Calm down." He looks away from me, out into the field.

I glance at Jareem. He's staring straight ahead, but I bet he's listening. Following the officer's gaze, I see the two cops who were searching out in the field. They're heading this way, flashlights zigzagging over the ground.

"So, you weren't here earlier?" The cop's looking at me again.

"Earlier? No, sir. I mean, yes, actually." I'm an idiot! "I was cleaning inside with Mr. Frogley. But, we finished and left."

"So, why'd you come back?"

"I heard all the sirens. Saw they were headed in this direction." My palms are sweating. "Just curious." Or should I have told the truth — said, *worried*? Admitted I remembered we forgot the chairs, and — no. Too complicated.

He nods, pulls a miniature black binder from his pocket. "I'll just get some particulars. What's your name?"

Shit. I lower my voice, hoping Jareem won't hear. "Sebastian."

"Last name?"

I hesitate and the cop squints up at me.

"Till."

"Phone?"

I give him Mrs. Ford's number.

The cop snaps his book shut, looks out to the field again. "Anything?" he calls.

"Yep." One of the cops, a woman, answers. She and the other cop are striding across the asphalt now. "We found a dog — grey, whippet-type thing. Only bigger."

Skinny! Found Skinny? I scan the asphalt. Then I glance back at Jareem. He lifts his chin, grins at me.

The lady cop stops beside me, so I'm standing between her and Jareem.

She tells the other cop, "When we found it, the poor thing couldn't have been dead for long."

Everything inside me liquefies.

"It was still warm. My guess?" she says. "One of those punks slit its gullet to get in some practice before the fight."

My stomach lurches into my throat. I barely stop myself from puking. Swallow vomit. Rage fills my lungs, burns through my whole body. I want to smash the cruiser window, rip Jareem's face off. I force myself to look away.

The cop who was quizzing me says, "*Gullet*, eh? You a Scrabble player?"

The lady cop snorts. "Yeah, right." For a moment, her flashlight shines in my face, making me flinch. "You okay, kid?"

I nod.

"You look kind of sick." She snaps her flashlight off, clips it onto her belt.

"Yeah. Well, that's sick." My voice sounds weird. Choked off. "I mean — what happened."

"Yes, it is. Seen worse, though."

I want to punch through that cruiser window. But I don't. Don't do anything.

"Better bag it," the first cop tells the lady cop. "And then go see if anyone knows who it belongs to." He looks up at me. "You hear anything about this evening, give me a call." He hands me a little card that I pocket without reading.

The other cop from the field slides into the driver seat of the police cruiser. As he pulls away, Jareem leers through the back window.

Alone in the quiet schoolyard, watching the cruisers leave, the total uselessness of my existence hits me like one of Jareem's punches. I stand there . . . and stand there . . . and stand . . . Every ounce of energy I have just keeping me from falling to my knees.

Walking home, I work on breathing. Try to spit the rancid taste from my mouth. Stifle an urge to kick the lights out of every parked car I pass.

Try not to picture Skinny.

Wonder what would have happened if I'd warned Mr. Frogley. Will he die because I didn't?

I'm almost home when I lurch into some bushes, crouch down low, and vomit.

Twenty-Four

"It's after nine o'clock, Seb," Mrs. Ford calls from the kitchen as I close the front door. "I wish you'd — What's happened?" she says when she steps into the hall and sees me.

"I'm sorry," I say, lurching toward the bathroom where I stick my head under the tap to rinse out my mouth and splash water on my face.

Mrs. Ford stands in the doorway and hands me a towel. "What's wrong?"

The top half of my head feels like it could explode so I squeeze it tight between my palms.

"Come with me."

I follow her back to the kitchen. She pours a glass of milk, but when she offers it I'm afraid I'll drop it, so I just shake my head.

"You're upset. You won't tell me why?"

I wrap my arms around my chest, try to clear my throat. "There was a fight. At Fairhaven. Mr. Frogley had a heart attack. I saw him when the ambulance took him away."

"Oh, no! Is — "

"And the guy who beat me up slit Skinny's throat. He's dead."

186

"I'm so sorry." Her face scrunches up like an empty lunch bag. "Are you going to be okay?"

"Yeah." I plunk down at the kitchen table. "Actually, no. What if Mr. Frogley dies, too?" I bury my head in my arms and suddenly, I'm bawling. I can't stop.

"Oh, Seb." Mrs. Ford puts a box of tissues on the table and rubs my back.

"Skinny's dead because of me."

"That's not true."

"And Mr. Frogley's going to die because of me."

"Now hold on, Seb. Why would you say that?" Mrs. Ford's voice catches. "They took him to hospital. We could call, if we knew which one."

I lift my head. "St. Joseph's."

"I'll call right now."

I blow my nose, wipe my palms over my eyes, try to stop the tears while I listen to Mrs. Ford dial the number at the little table in the hall. She waits a long time after telling whoever answers Mr. Frogley's name. Then she begs for a bit of information. "My son was with him when they put him in the ambulance. He's very upset now. We're practically like family."

Just for an instant, the wonder of Mrs. Ford calling me her son wipes out every other thought in my brain.

Then she says, "Thank you," hangs up, and steps back into the kitchen.

"He's in Intensive Care. They say his condition seems to be stabilizing and likely he'll be all right. But they'll be monitoring him constantly." She gives my back another pat then wraps her arms around my shoulders. "That's good, Seb."

I can't remember the last time anyone hugged me. I put one hand over hers. Manage to choke out, "Thank you."

⌒

I'm slumped at the opposite end of the couch from Mrs. Ford. We're watching the late-night news. I'm relieved that Fairhaven isn't on it, but I wonder — who called the ambulance? When a story about Greyhound racing comes on, Mrs. Ford changes the channel to some talk show. "This okay, Seb?"

I shrug. I really don't care.

I could have stopped it all from happening, could've told Mr. Frogley about the fight. He could've had a cop car there before anyone showed. None of it would have happened.

"Seb?"

"Huh?" I say, startled. "I mean, pardon?"

Mrs. Ford stands in the doorway. "I said, may I get you something? A cup of tea?"

"No, thanks."

She goes into the kitchen.

I've gotta quit screwing up. Start using my head more.

Mrs. Ford comes back into the living room with a mug and sits down on the couch again. "Seb, I wouldn't bring this up now, except that I can see you're still thinking about it." She sighs. "Some things aren't making much sense to me."

I sink even lower into the couch.

"Did you already know that something was supposed to happen at the school this evening?"

How would she know that? I look down at the flower pattern on the arm of the couch. She'll be pissed as hell with the truth. But a voice in my head is yelling, *Just tell her!*

And she already warned me — she doesn't like lies.

"Yeah." I glance at her face. Her eyebrows move up a bit, but I keep going. "Earlier today, that guy Don asked me if I wanted to be in his rumble."

"The boy I suggested you avoid?"

I nod, and her frown makes me feel even worse.

"Well," she finally says. "At least you knew to steer clear of him."

I blink. Try to lick my lips, but my tongue is too dry.

"Obviously, choosing *not* to fight was wise." She sips her tea.

"I should have told Mr. Frogley."

She nods. "Mm-hmm."

"And, if I'd stayed, Skinny might still be alive. Mr. Frogley might not be in hospital."

"Or both of you might be in hospital!" she says. "Seb, other than neglecting to inform Mr. Frogley, you didn't do anything wrong."

I can't look her in the eye. I focus on the couch's dumb pattern again, trace the outline of a lousy flower with my finger. Finally, I take a deep breath. "Not actually."

"Oh?" she says.

Still staring at the couch, I say, "I never 'steered clear' of Don. I was with him, and some other guys, the night I got wasted."

"I already know that."

"Yeah, but . . . I didn't tell Mr. Frogley about Don's fight because I didn't want him to know I hung around with any of those guys."

Mrs. Ford stares with wide eyes.

I suck in my breath. "The guy who killed Skinny and beat me up? He did that because I was supposed to be Don."

"What do you mean, you were *supposed to be Don*?" Her eyebrows are practically touching but she still doesn't sound mad.

I feel as though I just pressed the button for one of those wheelchair doors: you have to let them open all the way before they'll shut again. So, I tell her everything — what I did as payback for Don's bike. Why I probably got beaten up. And, just like those automatic doors swing open fast and smooth, the truth comes out quick, almost easy.

When I finish, she looks really old and tired. She takes a deep breath. "Well, Seb. I must say, I'm stunned. I just don't know what to think. And I'm not sure how we proceed from here. I appreciate your honesty. But . . . " She gazes up at the ceiling for a while before looking back at me. "Sorry, Seb. I've got to think." She stands up. "Okay?"

I nod.

She sighs and trudges out of the room.

Not sure how we proceed. Her bedroom door clicks shut.

I lie like a log on the couch. The knot in my gut is gone.

I'm completely hollow.

Twenty-Five

"What's wrong?" Nina asks at lunch the following Monday.

Matt pops his can of diet Coke open. "Seb feels sick just watching you eat that disgusting mess."

"Disgustingly delicious." Nina shoves another forkfull of poutine into her mouth and smacks her lips. "Seriously, Seb, what's going on?"

"Nothing." My jaw is sore from clenching it all weekend.

"You're clearly upset about something. For one thing, you haven't had a bite of lunch. Maybe Matty and I can help."

Matt sighs. "Nina's full of sh — " He pauses. "Shall we say, intuition."

"And grit," she adds, nodding, her hair a mass of bouncy springs.

"In other words, she'll badger you until you talk, Seb."

After taking a moment to psych myself, I tell them part of what happened Friday evening.

Matt says Mr. Frogley could have been due for a heart attack no matter what he'd been doing. That's what a doctor told his uncle after he had a heart attack jogging.

Wish I could believe that.

Then I tell them what happened to Skinny.

Nina drops her fork. "No!" She stares at me a moment, her mouth open, then presses her hands against her face and sobs quietly.

A few kids look our way as Matt pats her back and I rush to grab her a clean serviette.

After a minute, she looks up with red eyes. "Poor Skinny." She wipes her face. "Damn that creep. And damn Don, too."

I wait for her to say *I told you so,* but she doesn't.

Matt says, "That bastard Jareem should have his balls cut off."

Nina sighs. "Not a bad idea. But I suppose that's taking revenge too far, too. Does Mrs. Ford know all this?"

"Yeah."

"Who's Mrs. — "

"Later, Matty. So?"

"She said, *We'll take it one day at a time, for now.* And she's been making phone calls, but she hasn't said anything about giving me the boot. Yet."

"I'll keep all my fingers crossed for you." Nina holds up both hands to show me.

"So tell me, who's Mrs. Ford?" Matt says.

By the end of lunch, I still feel like shit, but somehow, sharing with Matt and Nina makes the load a little lighter.

⌒

Tuesday, I search through my locker for the lunch I threw in earlier. After finding out just before coming to school that I can visit Mr. Frogley, I'm hungry for the first time since Friday.

"Hey, Seb." Nina pulls a small bag out of her locker. "How are things going?"

"Still don't know what Mrs. Ford plans to do. But she got an update on Mr. Frogley. He's staying in hospital a few more days, and he needs some sort of heart pills; but mostly, he's doing fine."

"Phew! Anyway, I got you a gift." She holds out the bag.

With one glance I go from surprised to not. Inside the bag is my typical gift — one meant for somebody else. It's a little stuffed teddy bear in a red top. "Thanks. Cute."

Nina pulls it from the bag. "It's the message he's holding that's important. I stitched that part myself." Amazingly, she blushes. "It's from one of my favourite books."

I look closely at a small square of white cloth that I'd figured was a sales tag. Tiny, neat words read, *Promise me you'll always remember — You're braver than you believe, stronger than you seem, and smarter than you think.*

All at once, I recall being nestled beside Mom as she reads to me.

"That's great." I laugh, partly to cover the fact that I'm blinking back tears. "First time I've ever been compared to Winnie the Pooh, though."

She smiles. "No disrespect intended." Then she pulls another, bigger bag from her locker and says, "Time for lunch, and a little math assistance, please."

Matt arrives with his Coke and chips. "Nice teddy."

"Yep." I pop Winnie onto the shelf in my locker and go back to looking for my lunch.

"You should check out the animal shelter with Nina," Matt says.

"Drop it!" That came out meaner than I meant. "Sorry. But I don't want another dog."

"It's not just that!" Nina pulls a giant cookie from her bag. "You can volunteer and I bet they'd give you a paying job after a while."

"Maybe." I finally find my lunch. "Got it."

"Okay." Nina links elbows with Matt and me, then sings, "We're off to the cafeteria," to a *Wizard of Oz* tune. Matt and I don't budge.

"Come on, guys. We've got to skip."

Matt groans. "Sometimes you are the weirdest — "

I laugh.

"Sebastian, my man!" Don calls.

Nina drops our arms and mutters, *"Malaka."* Not sure what that means, but I'm pretty sure I agree.

Don elbows a couple of girls out of his way as he strides toward me.

"I'm not sticking around for this. Meet us at our table, Seb." Nina marches past Don muttering in Greek, with Matt close behind her.

Don plants himself in front of me. "So, Sebastian. Where've you been?"

I shrug.

"The fight didn't happen on Friday, but you still missed a good show." He takes a quick look around. "Things hardly got started when an old guy comes racing across the field yelling, *I've called the police.*"

"Oh?" I stare down the hall after Nina and Matt.

"Then, he almost trips over this dog that's splurting blood as it runs."

My throat muscles spasm.

"The guy looks at the dog, grabs his chest, and drops dead!" Don chuckles. "Serves the old fart right."

His words burn. *"Serves him right?"*

He shrugs. "He should have minded his own business."

My jaw seizes. I stop myself taking a swing at his smirk.

Glancing around again, he says, "Anyhow, the cops showed real fast. So, everyone took off. Except Sean."

And Jareem.

Don hangs his head, shakes it slowly. "Sean got cut bad . . . supposedly. I guess by the guy who chopped the dog. Cops took him to the hospital."

I don't say anything.

"Yeah," Don says. "He's still there. I went to see him yesterday. He's screwed up, man. Says he yelled for help but I ditched him." He shakes his head, rubbing his fingers over his chin. "That's total bullshit. If I'd heard him, I'd have helped. Besides, he could've scared that crazy guy off. Sean's a whack job. Who even cares about a fucking mutt? Wants to *get even* now — for what?"

Out of nowhere, Shanisse's voice sounds in my head. *You always do the same thing when you're lying.*

Donny's rubbing his chin, accusing Sean — the zombie — of bullshit.

We were in the tree belt . . . I couldn't breathe right. Donny was scratching his chin, saying he didn't think Carl would be waiting on Braemar.

He was lying. And he's lying now.

He lowers his voice, smiles. "Anyhow, before talking to me about it, the little asshole goes and tells the cops — " He looks along the hall.

Following his gaze, I see the vice-principal heading our way.

Don says, "Let's go."

I follow him down the hall, itching to share my new insight: I'm not the *lying, chickenshit coward.* You are! And

Nina was right. If the guy on Braemar had set me up, it would have been after I made the pickup.

Three little grade-niners walking in front of us stop me from saying anything.

"Anyhow," Don whispers when the kids turn away, "cops were at my place 'cause fuckin' Sean told them I planned the whole thing!" His smile isn't working — his top lip twitches. The fury in his eyes keeps me quiet.

"Can you fuckin' believe it?" he asks, slamming through the exit to the parking lot. "Plus, he got caught with a piece, and told them I gave it to him."

"A piece of what?"

The door closes behind us. "You know — a fuckin' piece." He aims his fingers at me like a gun. "He could've smoked the crazy dog guy, instead of getting cut up himself. And now he's trying to blame everything on me." He glances around. There's not another person in sight.

"A gun? You gave him a gun?"

He looks me right in the eye. "*I* didn't say that."

I want to race back into the school, find Matt and Nina, sit in a safe little corner of the cafeteria. Forget about telling Don he's a liar.

"Fuckin' Sean. And I called the ambulance."

I don't ask, *Why call an ambulance if you didn't know he was hurt?*

"So, listen Sebastian. Seb, my man." He smiles, a tight, desperate-looking grimace. "You gotta do me a little favour. No biggie. And I'll pay you back." He glances around the parking lot again. "I'll give you some goodies."

"I don't want anything."

His eyes narrow. "Whatever. I told my old lady I was hanging with you on Friday. She remembered you from

Little League. She thinks you're a *nice boy*. When the cops came calling, she told them I couldn't have had anything to do with anything because I was with you." He smiles. "So, buddy, *if* the cops ask — they probably won't bother, but they've got your name now — tell them we were together. Say we went to the mall. Okay?"

"You gave the cops my name?"

His mouth twists into a sneer. "Chill, man! You won't get in trouble."

My heart is beating double-time. "It won't work."

He steps closer. "So, I can count on you, right?"

"I said, *it won't work.*" I'm talking loud and fast. "The cops already know I was at the school."

"What are you talking about?" Don's face flushes. "You weren't there. *I* was there. Are you trying to fuck with me?"

"No! I got there later. The cops took my name."

A muscle in his jaw twitches. "You lousy fucking liar. If I get in trouble because of you . . . " He plants a hand on my chest, shoves me back against the metal door.

Feels like my ribs are going to crack again. Rage grows with the pain.

"Why didn't you tell me you were going? I knew you were lying, you useless piece of shit."

I swat his hand away. "I'm telling you now. And I've got something else to tell you." I shove my face an inch from his. "You're the lousy, stinkin', chickenshit liar!"

He slams his palm onto my chest again and pulls his other fist back, aiming it at my face. I don't move a muscle. Then, his voice scarily calm and controlled, he says, "You better watch yourself, Sebastian!" He lowers his raised fist and lets go of my chest. "You wouldn't want

197

the cops to find out that you've had anything to do with
the business."

"What's that supposed to mean?"

He glances over his shoulder before turning to me
again. "I get in shit, so do you."

"I'll say I didn't know why that guy owed you money.
Helping a *buddy* collect on a debt isn't a crime."

"As if you didn't know what was really in that package."

I want to turn off, forget Geoff's warning, my own
suspicions. "I didn't. I don't."

Don sneers. "You are so pathetic. Crystal meth. Ecstasy.
Crack. You had it all in your pocket, delivery boy." He
yanks the door open, whacking me on the shoulder with
it. "I'm not going down," he says and strides back into the
school.

I go to rub my shoulder, discover the lunch bag still
clutched in my hand and let it drop.

I feel as though I'm falling backwards, into a deep,
dark hole. Twisting and turning. Out of control.

I head home, my feet on autopilot.

My whole body is vibrating. Like I've been zapped at
the core.

Everyone who warned me about Don was right. How
could I not see that? Me, the poster boy for fucked-up
foster families. I should've known all along.

I finally get Mrs. Ford — someone really decent — and
what do I do? Totally screw it up!

He's going to do whatever he can to protect himself.
The police are coming around for sure now. My heart
thuds in my ears. If Mrs. Ford didn't know how we'd
proceed before, she will now. I'll get kicked out. Wish I'd
punched his head in.

No. That's not using my head.

I'll tell the cops what Don told me about Sean's gun. Maybe I can prove Don's a liar. If he fries me, I'll lose my year. Have to change schools again. Probably won't even finish high school 'cause I'll be in juvie or some lousy group home till I'm out and on my own at eighteen. Forget those scholarships, forget college, for —

A horn blares. Brakes screech. A car stops so close, I touch its hood and feel its heat.

"I could've killed you!" the driver, her face chalk white, screams out the window.

Looks like she still could. I peer around, surprised to find I stepped off the curb without even noticing.

"Sorry! I'm sorry." I stumble to the sidewalk, then trudge the rest of the way home. Without Skinny.

Home is the same as always, with its matching front curtains, tidy porch, and freshly painted look. It's hard to believe I ever worried that Mrs. Ford might be like Psycho-Dad.

I wander around to the backyard and gaze at the bed I helped plant. This morning, I was the first to notice some new blooms on the 'forced' flowers.

I'm a good worker. Mr. Frogley always said so. I can get a job, maybe even finish high school, and then get my own place. I'm gonna be okay.

So, why do I feel like I'm back in that skate park, waiting for Carl, Jareem, and Big T to kill me?

Twenty-Six

"Just tell them what you told me." In the passenger seat, Mrs. Ford stares through swishing wipers. Looking between the front seats, I see her foot pushing at imaginary pedals as though she's the one driving, not Hassles.

Hassles bobs her head in agreement.

"I will. But telling the truth hasn't helped so far." If it had, I wouldn't be pretzelled in the back of this car right now. "Is the police station much further?" I look up at the black clouds blowing across the sky.

"Five minutes," Hassles says. "And would you please stop clicking that seat belt? It's getting on my nerves."

"Huh?" I glance down at the metal fastener in my hand. "Sorry."

Mrs. Ford looks back. "The police will see through that Donny's story eventually."

"I hope. But Matt says Don can spin lies faster than a spider on speed." And my story's so lame.

"Well, at least they didn't waste any time with that thug." Mrs. Ford looks out her window, and I wonder if she's thinking about Skinny.

"Who's that?" Hassles asks.

"I told you about him." Mrs. Ford sighs. "The one who attacked Seb, but got caught for something else? He's twenty-one, and already had a long list of prior offences. Apparently he's already in jail now for at least four years."

Hassles shakes her head. "Well," she says, "if nothing else, I hope Seb's finally learned his lesson."

Mrs. Ford doesn't say anything. Just keeps looking through her window. I wish she'd ask, *What lesson?* That you should avoid being ambushed? That everyone but me was right about Don all along? What?

Finally, I say, "Lesson, Ms. Haslett?"

"Play with the pigs, you're bound to get dirt on you."

"Oh," I say. "*That* lesson." I could almost laugh. Except for Jim and Betty and Mrs. Ford, CSC has always — supposedly without a clue — thrown me into stinkin' pigpens.

Mrs. Ford looks at Hassles. "A lot of young people make mistakes."

Hassles doesn't say another word. Mrs. Ford goes back to watching the traffic.

The rain has stopped. The wipers squeal across the glass. Hassles turns them off. "Looks like the sun wants to come out."

If Don gets away with his lies, I'll end up in juvie. I picture the guy with the stitches down his face from the last time I was in court. It's getting hard to breathe back here. I've gotta try to think positive. What did Geoff say the other day when we were in the backyard doing tae kwon do?

You're not going to need these moves. Sean's one seriously disillusioned disciple.

What do you mean? I asked after finishing my round-house kick.

You know where that went — right? Judas? Jesus? Geoff stared up at the sky. *Okay, sorry. Bad analogy.* He looked back at me. *Basically, I don't think Don's getting off the hook, or that you're going anywhere.*

I wonder. We crawl from one red light to the next. I watch a lone raindrop pushed by the wind make its jagged journey across my window.

I wish I'd had the guts to just come out and ask Mrs. Ford: *if we're 'taking it one day at a time,' when does my time run out?* I've pushed the question to the back of my mind so often that the back of my mind is overflowing with it.

I take a deep breath, "What happens if — I mean when . . . That is, *if* the police don't believe me and . . . " I clear my throat. "What I mean is, what happens — *if* I go to juvie — when I get out?"

Hassles stops for a red light. "The police haven't even charged you with anything yet."

Yet.

"Personally, I doubt they'll be able to gather enough evidence." Her nails tap on the steering wheel. "Especially since what you've told Mrs. Ford and me is the truth, right?" She stops tapping.

"Right. But I mean . . . " I swallow.

Mrs. Ford looks back. Squints. "Are you all right?"

I nod. "I just mean . . . " I look at her kind, wrinkled face. "You've only known me for five months."

Hassles says, "Don't worry. You'll remain a ward of the state until you're eighteen."

Is that supposed to make me feel good? "It's just that I . . . " I'm afraid to hear Mrs. Ford's answer, but

I've got to ask. "The thing is, I've already said so many goodbyes — not that I haven't wanted to leave sometimes — it's just . . . "

Mrs. Ford is still looking at me. "Oh, Sebastian."

I stare into her eyes.

Hassles says, "Now, Seb — "

"I want another chance, Mrs. Ford — with you."

She blinks and presses her lips together. It reminds me of Ms. Burk's look after I got pounded.

"Please."

"Seb, I'm getting old, so I don't want to make any big promises." She pauses.

I hold my breath waiting for her next words.

"But, I think you've got a good heart as well as a good shot at college. And if you're finished with the lies and omissions — "

"I am."

She smiles. "Then, I'd be willing to have you live with me again."

"Thanks, Mrs. Ford." My voice wobbles. "I promise I won't be any more trouble."

She reaches back and grabs my hand, her eyes fixed solid on mine. "So you're stuck with me for at least a few more years." She squeezes my hand a moment, then lets it go and faces forward.

At least *a few.* She's keeping me past eighteen! It's like a wall inside me bursts. I can't stop the rush of relief that floods through me. I'm glad I'm packed into the back where no one's watching as my body turns to putty. I swallow, stare through my window, and take a deep breath.

No matter what comes next, I've got a home.